LUNA STATION
QUARTERLY

Issue 029 | March 2017

Editor-in-Chief

Jennifer Lyn Parsons

Assistant Editors

Tara Calaby • Cathrin Hagey • Dana Mele
Andi Marquette • Megan Patton
Danielle Perry • Iona Sharma

LUNA STATION PRESS
NEW JERSEY

Luna Station Quarterly publishes short fiction on March 1st, June 1st,
September 1st, and December 1st. For more information and submission
guidelines, please visit our website at lunastationquarterly.com

For Luna Station Press

Creative Director–Tara Quinn Lindsey

Editor-in-Chief & Founder–Jennifer Lyn Parsons

LUNA STATION PRESS

576 Valley Road #197
Wayne, NJ 07470

www.lunastationpress.com

info@lunastationpress.com

CONTENTS

Editorial

Jennifer Lyn Parsons

A pixel-slinger and code monkey by trade, Jennifer is a life-long lover of story with a capital S. Her work has been seen in various magazines and she has published three books, with quite a few more in her back pocket. She counts Jim Jarmusch and Laura Ingalls Wilder as two of her biggest influences. Make of that what you will.

When not writing either code or fiction, she reads books and comics, and sometimes makes things out of wool or paper. She finds joy in making things, be they digital or analog.

I almost subtitled this editorial "The Queering of LSQ", but I felt it might be going a bit over the top. Despite our gorgeous cover (by the talented Priscilla Kim) and more than one story featuring a queer character, LSQ is not suddenly becoming an "LGBTQIA+ Literary Magazine". Truth be told, it's been that way for a long time without me saying or doing anything. It's been a natural progression and opening that's quietly made me happy as it's unfolded.

When I started this little magazine in 2009, I was a pretty different person and the world was a pretty different place. I was heavily closeted even to myself, gay marriage was not on the table, and I was filling the most immediate and visible need before me: making sure women's voices are heard. And so I've chosen to publish women writers exclusively. To clarify, if you tell me you identify with the woman end of the gender spectrum in a significant way, there is a place for you here.

That mission, that purpose hasn't changed. I'm just taking the moment right now, as the world gets rougher by the day, to stick a flag in the ground for queer characters and the queer authors who write for us. (We can argue my use of the word "queer" some other time, yeah?) We need these stories, just as we need stories featuring characters of various races and immigration status. They're all good, important stories.

But here's the interesting thing. These stories I'm talking about in this issue? They're not about being gay. In some cases, the love story and the characters' orientation are incidental, just as it would be if the characters were straight. There are no coming out stories, these women know who they are and are simply acting on that same impulse of attraction that their heterosexual counterparts would. That's part of what makes them so all good, so universal. That whole "representation" thing you've heard so much about? This is what it looks like.

These stories are not about waving flags, shouting from the mountain tops, or shoving anything down anyone's throat. They're actually about superheroes and magic and strange bubbles of time. As with all good characters and good stories, they stand on their own merit. They transport us and, much of the time, both gender and sexuality become incidental to the weaving of a good yarn. Swap Han Solo's gender and Star Wars doesn't become a gay story when she and Leia fall in love, right? It's still the same story. There just would happen to be a couple of gay characters in there. (Poe Dameron, Space Gay. Fingers crossed. That's all I'm saying.)

The thing is, the world is changing. Things were getting better for everyone for a while. Now we're hitting the backlash. That's when stories become more important than ever. That's when diversity and representation and the voices of minorities need to be heard more than ever. And at the same time, LSQ is not a purposefully political magazine. Whatever else goes on, a good story is the most important thing we publish. It's a chance to uplift and entertain and provide a refuge from all the rotten crap going on around us.

Stories allow us to escape for a little while, to dream of better times and better places. Stories allow us to hope and hope is needed now more than any time in my own memory. For many of our authors and readers, getting the chance to see themselves reflected back in the stories they read can make all the difference. For them, and for myself, one girl taking another girl's hand and looking at her with love is exactly the kind of respite we need from a world that feels more and more unwelcoming. For all of us, that's what hope looks like.

LSQ|028

How Lady Nightmare Stole Captain Alpha's Girlfriend

Kristen Brand

If Kristen Brand could have any superpower, she'd want telekinesis so she wouldn't have to move from her computer to pour a new cup of tea. She spends far too much time on the internet, and when she's not writing, she's usually reading novels or comic books. To find out more about her work and read her free online superhero serial, visit kristenbrand.com.

The last time Sara had been held hostage had definitely been worse.

Last time, the hostage-taker had been an angry man in a ski mask. He'd shouted at her to hand over all the cash in her register, his face so close that she could count every vessel in his bloodshot eyes. She'd been in the middle of giving it to him, the bills sticking to her sweaty hands, when the police had appeared. The thief had grabbed her and waved his gun, shouting that he'd shoot her if they got too close. She'd been a crying, terrified mess for the entire two-hour standoff. Then Captain Alpha had come and put an end to it, and all in all, it had been the worst day of her life.

Today would probably be a close second, though, because this time her hostage-taker was a supervillain.

"There." The supervillain finished tying the rope around Sara's ankles and stood up. "How's that? Not cutting off your circulation, is it?"

Sara sat in an armchair in her own apartment. (That was the only part worse than last time. She'd barely managed to go back to work without having a panic attack; now she was going to feel terrified in her own home.) Her wrists were bound behind her back in the same elaborate, looping knots that now tied her ankles. Instead of answering the question, she looked at the floor.

"Alright. But let me know if your hands or feet start feeling tingly. I'll loosen it. Promise."

Lady Nightmare. Sara was ninety percent sure the woman standing in front of her was Lady Nightmare. Or maybe Bella Morte? Sara didn't watch the news enough to keep all the various supervillains of the world straight. Whoever she was, she wore a dapper three-piece suit, domino mask, and fedora all a shade of purple so dark it was nearly black. She had fair skin and dark hair cut in a classic bob, and she smelled like raspberries. That last bit probably wasn't the most relevant thing to notice about a masked villain who'd broken into your apartment, but she'd gotten really close when she'd tied Sara to the chair, okay? Sara couldn't *not* notice.

The supervillain picked up Sara's cell phone, and the four-digit password jumped to the front of Sara's mind. Apparently, the supervillain could read minds. Because that wasn't terrifying at all. And both Lady Nightmare and Bella Morte had that superpower, so it didn't even help Sara figure out who'd captured her.

Sara could only hear half of the conversation that followed, but it was one she'd been afraid of ever since Captain Alpha had asked her out. It was all "I have your girlfriend" and "Come alone if you want to see her again" and stuff like that. Captain Alpha probably said something macho in response, but the supervillain hung up on him. "That went well." She set down the phone and beamed at Sara. "Anyway, don't worry about a thing. I've no intention of hurting *you*. I mean, yeah, I might have to do my nightmare thing to you to give him a bit of extra motivation, but you'll be fine."

Sara's stomach tied itself into a knot as elaborate as the ones around her limbs. "Nightmare thing?" she asked, her voice squeaking.

"Yeah, you know. I'm Lady Nightmare. I get into your head telepathically? Make you live out your worst fear? It's my whole thing."

Oh.

Well, at least Sara knew who'd taken her hostage now.

"You'll be fine," Lady Nightmare said with a dismissive wave. "Got anything to drink around here?"

Sara didn't drink, so no, but she couldn't say anything as Lady Nightmare strolled into her kitchen. Oh, crap, her kitchen. There must be at least two days' worth of dirty dishes in the sink, and when was the last time she'd taken out the trash? If Sara had known someone would be breaking into her home today, she would have cleaned. This was going to be awful. Once Lady Nightmare was finished (assuming Sara survived), the apartment would be crawling with cops, and they'd all get a good look at the dirty clothes on her bedroom floor, piles of unopened mail on the kitchen table, and a floor she hadn't vacuumed in weeks. They were going to look at her all judgmentally, and it was going to be awful. Maybe the nightmare thing would kill her and spare her the mortification.

"This is really good. Did you make it?"

Lady Nightmare was leaning against the bar between the kitchen and living room, holding a fork in one hand and a green Tupperware in the other.

"No." The word came out softly and weakly, but Sara was

actually pretty miffed, thank you very much. That was her mother's baklava in that Tupperware.

"Well, it's really good." Lady Nightmare took another bite, and the fork lingered between her lips as she savored the taste. They were full, glossy lips, her lipstick a shade of deep plum that matched her outfit and complimented her pale skin. The fork slid slowly and sensuously out, and Sara tore her gaze away, heart pounding.

Stop staring, she instructed herself. Lady Nightmare had to be doing that on purpose. No one was naturally that sexy when they ate.

"So, how come Captain Alpha is in your phone as 'Captain Alpha' and not his real name?" Lady Nightmare asked.

Sara had to swallow before she could answer. "He hasn't told me his real name. He said... What did he say? He said knowing his secret identity would put both of us in danger or something."

Lady Nightmare snorted. "What a douchebag."

You don't know the half of it, Sara thought. Then she had another thought that was much worse. Captain Alpha was coming here. To her apartment. She didn't want him in her apartment. What if he defeated Lady Nightmare? He'd rescue Sara *again*, and he'd be so damn pleased with himself, and her bedroom was right over there, and—no. That wasn't going to happen. That *probably* wasn't going to happen. There was a better chance of Lady Nightmare just killing them both. Yes, that was it. Sara just had to think positively.

Lady Nightmare finished the baklava and gave herself a tour of Sara's apartment. She browsed through Sara's bookshelves ("Oh, I've always wanted to read this one. I heard it's really good."), glanced over framed family photographs, and shook up Sara's collection of snow globes. Sara kept her eyes on the wall and definitely didn't pay attention to the way Lady Nightmare's soft-looking lips pursed thoughtfully as she gazed at Sara's paintings.

How long before Captain Alpha got here? How long before Lady Nightmare made Sara live out her worst fear? Sara wondered what it would be. She was afraid of heights, and she'd had night-mares before about falling off a building. Could Lady Nightmare make her feel pain? Because Sara was definitely afraid of being tortured to death. She'd once dated a guy who dragged her to awful horror movies showing graphic stuff like that. Though none of those dates had been as bad as the one she'd had with Captain Alpha.

It had been at a fancy Italian restaurant two days ago, and he'd started it off by ordering wine even though Sara protested that she didn't drink. And then he'd talked. He'd talked and talked and talked. No awkward silences on this first date. Sara had smiled and nodded at first, but eventually she'd stopped, trying to politely hint that she wasn't interested in hearing about how the entire backstage staff had begged for his autograph the last time he'd been interviewed on late night TV. The date had lasted less than two hours in reality, but it had felt like at least five.

If only it had ended there, but *everyone* she knew had asked how it'd went afterward. And when Sara had answered not so great, a lot of their replies had been "But he's saved so many people," "But he's so handsome," or "But he's a superhero." Like he could never do anything wrong, and it was Sara's fault for not having a good time.

"I like this one. Where'd you get it?" Lady Nightmare pulled Sara from her thoughts. She was pointing at Sara's favorite one of her paintings: a moody mermaid under a starry sky.

"Made it," Sara mumbled, lowering her gaze to the floor.

"What was that?"

"It's one of mine," Sara tried again, less mumbly. "I painted it."

"What? No way!" Lady Nightmare looked around the room again, her eyes lighting up behind the mask. She'd been pretty before, but the genuine delight on her face made her stunning. "Are all of these yours? That's—" Her phone buzzed. She pulled it out of her suit jacket pocket and put it to her ear. "Got it. Thanks."

She pocketed her phone and turned back to Sara, the smile gone from her face. Sara had liked her a lot better when she'd been smiling.

"Captain Alpha just showed up," Lady Nightmare said. "I'm gonna have to do my thing now."

"Your nightmare thing," Sara said weakly.

"Yeah..." Lady Nightmare approached slowly and knelt in front of Sara's chair. "I won't lie. This is gonna suck. But it'll be over soon, and it's not real, okay? Just remember it's not real."

Sara nodded mutely. Her mouth was suddenly very dry. She tried to prepare herself, but she had no idea what was coming. Would it be a horror movie monster or something much more realistic and vile? The most fear she'd ever felt before was when she'd been cowering on the filthy tile floor of the store, the man in the ski mask screaming at the police outside. She didn't want to relive that, either. Lady Nightmare's mouth was curved in an attractive frown. Was she hesitating or just concentrating on using her powers? Wouldn't it be nice if—

Sara was standing in the church she used to go to with her

parents when she'd been younger. It looked bigger and darker than she remembered, and the saints in the icons on the walls had shadowed faces and grim eyes. Sara's wedding dress was tight and scratchy, and Captain Alpha stood next to her. A strange priest asked, "Do you take this man to be your lawfully wedded husband—"

"No," Sara tried to say, but no sound came out of her mouth. This wasn't right. This wasn't happening. This wasn't even a proper Orthodox wedding ceremony.

"Of course she does," said Captain Alpha, flashing a smile of perfect white teeth.

Sara tried to pull away, but his hand gripped her arm, and she couldn't budge. She twisted around, looking pleadingly at the congregation for someone who could help her. She didn't recognize anyone. Where were her parents? Where were her friends? The strangers all smiled at her. Why couldn't they see this was wrong?

Then Sara wasn't in the church anymore. She was in her bedroom, and Captain Alpha was there, too.

"No," Sara said, shaking her head back and forth.

"You'll like it. Trust me." It was the same thing he'd said when he'd ordered her wine at the restaurant. And the worst part was he honestly believed it. The possibility that Sara wouldn't—that any woman wouldn't—had never crossed his mind.

Sara couldn't move. She couldn't breathe. He came closer and closer, and she couldn't do anything. Her bedroom—her homey, familiar bedroom hadn't changed, but something about it looked so sinister now. She had to escape. If she didn't get away, she'd never escape this moment for the rest of her life. And no one would ever believe her, because he was a *hero*, and nobody wanted to believe bad things about their heroes. *Run. Scream. Do something before it's too late!* But it was already too late. He reached her and—

Sara was back in her living room, tied up in her chair and gasping for breath.

"Shit," said Lady Nightmare. "I'm such an asshole. Oh my God. Are you okay?"

Sara didn't know. Her heart was pounding so hard it almost hurt.

"Forget this." Lady Nightmare yanked at the knot around Sara's ankles and untied her. "I thought you were going to be afraid of spiders or something. Are you okay? I'm so sorry."

And Sara was officially so pathetic that she'd made a supervillain feel bad for her. This was a new low.

"You're not pathetic," said Lady Nightmare. How had she—oh, right. Mind-reading. "You're not," she repeated. "I'm just an unbelievable jackass. I didn't think— Here. Lean forward."

Sara leaned forward so Lady Nightmare could untie her arms. Her shirt stuck to her back, which had gotten soaked with sweat over the course of her nightmare. She must smell so gross right now. Lady Nightmare's fingers brushed Sara's arms as she expertly untied the ropes, and Sara probably would have taken a secret, guilty enjoyment out of how close they were if it weren't for the lingering nightmare-related terror.

The ropes fell away, and Lady Nightmare straightened up. "There. Are you— No, you're not okay. I don't know why I keep asking that. Shit." She stood there for a moment that probably wasn't as long as it seemed. Sara ran her hands up and down her freed arms absently, even though the ropes hadn't hurt.

"Right." Lady Nightmare rubbed the back of her neck and looked briefly away. "Well, I'll go fight Captain Alpha outside or something. You just...stay here. Sorry again."

She winced, took about three steps in the direction of the door, then stopped herself and turned back around. "Why are you even dating him?"

Sara jerked. That had sounded a lot like an accusation.

"Sorry," Lady Nightmare said again. "I didn't mean— You don't have to answer that. It's none of my business."

She turned to leave.

"No, I—" Sara wasn't sure she wanted Lady Nightmare to leave yet. But on the other hand, she felt an undeniable relief that the supervillain *would* leave if Sara wanted her to. "He saved my life. There was this guy with a gun who tried to rob the place where I work, and Captain Alpha—he saved my life. He asked me out right after—in front of the police and the reporters and everyone. I didn't know how to say no with so many people watching."

"And I'm guessing your *date* was just him telling you how awesome he is and how everyone who doesn't like him is a moron?"

Sara smiled gratefully. Finally, someone who understood. "Exactly. It's like being a prick is his superpower. But he... I tried to tell him. When dinner was over I said he was nice enough but I just didn't feel any chemistry and...." Sara sighed, feeling that awful sense of helplessness closing in on her from every side again. "He just steamrolled right over me. He said he was a man with many sides and it would take time to get to know all of him, and that he was taking me to a basketball game next. Last time I went out with someone who couldn't take a hint, I just ignored her calls afterward, but...."

"Captain Alpha doesn't let people ignore him," Lady Nightmare finished.

"Right..." Sara slumped in her chair. She felt whiny and pathetic. "I should have, I don't know, been firmer or something. It's my own fault."

"No." Lady Nightmare crossed the distance between them and crouched down so that she was at Sara's eye level. Her eyes were deep brown, nearly black, and she had the longest eyelashes. "Don't blame yourself for—"

The front door burst off its hinges with a bang. Sara flinched, and Lady Nightmare spun around while pulling a gun from her jacket.

The gun was ripped from her hand. It flew through the air like someone had tied an invisible string around it and yanked. That was Captain Alpha. He was telekinetic, which meant he could move things with his mind. He'd told Sara over dinner that only people with the greatest mental discipline could control such a power.

Sara had her doubts.

"It's alright now, Sara," he proclaimed. "I'm here."

He was good-looking. That was the only positive thing she had to say about him. With perfectly styled sandy hair, a handsome face, and a body that must have taken hours with a personal trainer everyday to maintain, he looked exactly like a stereotypical hero. And while listening to him drone on about himself over dinner had ruined his mystique, Sara couldn't deny he had charisma at times. The way he stood in the doorway with his hands on his hips radiated enough confidence to trick you into thinking his garish costume looked good.

Lady Nightmare charged him, but Captain Alpha thrust out his hand and stopped her with a jolt. He didn't have to touch her. It was like she hit an invisible barrier.

"That's close enough," he said. "I'd rather keep some distance between me and the range of your powers."

He flicked his wrist, and Lady Nightmare went flying back. She slammed into the wall with such force that it knocked down two of Sara's paintings. A pained grunt escaped her lips, and Sara cringed. This was all her fault. She'd distracted Lady Nightmare with her stupid problems, letting Captain Alpha take her off guard.

"You made a mistake coming here." Captain Alpha's voice was brave and bold, but he took no steps closer to Lady Nightmare pinned against the wall. "Did you really think I wouldn't save her?"

Lady Nightmare didn't answer. She looked like she was having trouble just breathing. Her feet were inches above the floor. How much pressure must Captain Alpha be putting on her to keep her like that? And how could she escape? Captain Alpha didn't look like he was going to get close enough for her to use her superpowers.

"*Sara.*"

She jerked at the sound of her name. The way Captain Alpha said it made her think he'd already called her a few times without her noticing. Once he had her attention, though, he gave her a winning smile. "This has been an eventful week for you, hasn't it? Good thing I'm around to keep you out of trouble."

Sara's mouth opened, but no words came out. Lady Nightmare, however, managed to growl, "Fuck you."

An ugly expression came over Captain Alpha's face, and it felt like the air pressure in the room changed. Lady Nightmare gasped in pain, and the plaster on the wall around her cracked. Captain Alpha's telekinesis had just hit her like a hammer.

"That's enough from you," he said. "You came after my girlfriend. I don't think anyone will object if I use a little more force than necessary to bring you in."

"No!" Sara jumped to her feet, only then realizing that she'd been sitting frozen in her chair like an idiot the whole time.

"It's okay, Sara," Captain Alpha said in what he probably thought was a comforting tone. "I won't let her hurt you."

I'm not afraid of her, I'm afraid of you! she shouted in her head. What she said aloud was, "N-no. She didn't hurt me. You... You don't have to—"

"This is too much for you. I understand. Why don't you go into another room and wait? I'll come get you when I'm done here." He winked.

"I..." She what? What could she possibly do here that would make any difference? She looked at Lady Nightmare, her beautiful lips twisted in an agonized grimace. Their gazes met, and Sara ached like she was the one who'd been slammed into the wall.

"Go on, now." Captain Alpha jerked his head in the direction of the hallway. "I'll take care of this."

It was that damned confidence in his voice. The authority had Sara's feet moving to the hallway before she even knew what she was doing. Maybe Lady Nightmare could escape on her own? She was a supervillain, right? A real one, not one of those wackos who got high and tied a blanket around their necks before breaking into a liquor store. She must deal with this kind of thing all the time. Or, wait, somebody had called Lady Nightmare to tell her when Captain Alpha showed up at the apartment. She had a lookout. Maybe that person would help her. Supervillains always had minions, right? She'd be okay. It wouldn't matter if Sara left.

Sara's legs were shaking. She walked slowly past Captain Alpha, who smiled encouragingly. Nobody would blame her. She didn't have powers. What was she supposed to do? She couldn't even stand up for herself when it came to ordering drinks at dinner. And even if she did do something—something ineffectual and stupid, probably—she'd be helping a supervillain. That wasn't what you were supposed to do in a situation like this. You were supposed to cheer for the hero and fall in love with him for rescuing you.

This was all the man in the ski mask's fault. If only he hadn't tried to rob the store while she'd been there, Sara would never have met Captain Alpha and this never would have happened. If she ever saw that jerk again, she was going to kick him in the balls. Except she wouldn't, because she never did anything that brave in real life. She just went along with what people expected of her, even when it left her with the worst hero ever. And now she was going to walk away and let him hurt Lady Nightmare— whom Sara felt a stronger connection with than the man she was supposedly dating, despite the fact that she'd broken into Sara's apartment and tied her to a chair. Sara didn't know if that said more about her own weird turn-ons or Captain Alpha's complete and utter failure as a date or even a decent human being, but it didn't matter, because at the end of the night she'd still be stuck with him, and—no. Screw this.

Sara grabbed one of the snow globes from the shelf to her right and chucked it at Captain Alpha's fat head.

She didn't have the greatest aim, so it hit his shoulder instead. He flinched and spun around. "Sara?"

"Get out of my apartment," she said. "I'm breaking up with you. We're done."

"What?"

"You heard me. Put down Lady Nightmare and get out. And stop calling me."

Captain Alpha's mouth had been hanging open in confusion, but it snapped shut and he smiled. "Sara, listen to me. Lady Nightmare is using mind-control on you. This isn't what you want."

"No! I'm not being mind-controlled. The fact that you think that's the only explanation is—argh!" She grabbed fist-fulls of her hair. "I tried to be nice about this and let you down easy after dinner, but you didn't get the hint, so I can't be nice anymore. I don't want to date you! I don't know how I can get any clearer than that."

His mouth twisted, and it made Sara want to run and hide. He was frightening. How did people not see how frightening he was? Did the flashy costume and handsome smile make everyone forget he could kill them with a thought?

"Wait in the other room," he said through clenched teeth. "We'll talk about this later."

She took a deep breath. It was too late to stop now. "There's nothing to talk about. I don't like you like that."

"I saved your life! How can you not like me?"

"And thank you for saving me. I really mean it. But that doesn't mean I'm obligated to go on a second date with you. Do you make everyone you save go out with you?"

"No, but that's the point!" He'd turned almost completely away from Lady Nightmare. If he would just loosen his mental grip on her.... "I chose you out of everyone. You should be flattered!"

Sara swallowed. "I'm sorry. It's just not working out."

"You like toying with me, don't you? I hope you're enjoying yourself."

"What?!"

He turned his back completely on Lady Nightmare, his cape flaring out behind him before flapping back down. "I did everything I could for you, and you're throwing it back in my face."

"We went on *one* date. You—I can't believe you—" Sara snatched up another snow globe and flung it at him. "Get over yourself!"

He should have ducked, but apparently his instincts were to use his powers. His hand swung up, palm out, and the globe stopped in mid-air a foot from his face.

At the exact same moment, Lady Nightmare dropped to the floor and landed lithely on her feet. He couldn't focus his powers on more than one thing at a time. So much for mental discipline.

Captain Alpha's eyes widened. "Oh, shit." The snow globe plummeted, and he swung around to face Lady Nightmare again. But as soon as she'd hit the floor, she'd sprinted at him. Sara cringed, expecting him to slam Lady Nightmare into the wall again. But he stumbled back like he'd been hit, though Lady Nightmare hadn't touched him. Lady Nightmare's sprint slowed to a stop a second later, and she smiled wickedly. Then Captain Alpha fell to his knees.

"No, no, no, no," he gasped, shaking his head back and forth. He curled into a ball on the floor, jerking and twitching. His eyes darted this way and that, staring fearfully at things Sara couldn't see.

That nightmare thing sure packed a punch.

"Are you okay?" Lady Nightmare walked past Captain Alpha like he wasn't even there and stopped in front of Sara, looking her quickly up and down.

"Me? What about you?"

"Eh, I've taken worse hits than that."

Sara glanced at Captain Alpha cowering on the floor, unable to still the tremors shaking her body. Was it really over? "What happens now?" she asked.

Lady Nightmare glanced back at him, too. "I won't kill him, if that's what you're worried about. I'll let him enjoy his nightmare a while longer. He thinks he's lost his powers and is getting creatively tortured by all his greatest enemies. By the time I let him go, he'll be too traumatized to ever fight crime again. Though he'll probably keep doing publicity tours."

Sara nodded like this was perfectly normal, like supervillains told her their evil plots all the time. She probably would have nodded along even if Lady Nightmare had spoken complete gibberish, as long as her tone was reassuring.

Lady Nightmare took Sara's hand, and Sara's gaze snapped to the dark eyes staring out at her from under the mask. "I need you to wait ten minutes after I leave, then call the cops," Lady Nightmare said. "If you don't, they'll suspect you. Tell them what happened, and be mostly honest. Act confused and scared, and they'll assume I used mind-control on you. Can you do that?"

"I think so." Sara's gaze dropped to Lady Nightmare's stylish shoes. Her hand went limp, and Lady Nightmare let it slip away. "But you didn't... I mean you..."

"No, that was all you. I was too far away to control you when you threw stuff at him. Thanks for that, by the way. You were awesome."

But Sara hadn't been thinking about the moment when she'd become an accessory to a crime. She was thinking about the smell of raspberries and how Lady Nightmare's kissable lips wouldn't leave her mind. Wait, was Lady Nightmare gay? She was, wasn't she? Or was that Bella Morte? Dang it, Sara really should've paid more attention to supervillains on the news. This was important.

Lady Nightmare grinned. "Bella Morte's straight as a board. I'm the gay one."

Sara could feel her cheeks heating. "Oh! Um...."

"And I wasn't using mind-control for that, either. Anyway, I can't make people do something completely out of character. Take Captain Douchebag back there." She jabbed a thumb in Captain Alpha's direction. "I can't make him graciously accept your decision to turn him down. But I *can* convince him to dump you and tell everyone that he's letting you go to protect you from his enemies, because he's just so self-sacrificing and noble."

Sara wouldn't have been surprised if she developed the power to fly on the spot. "Really?"

"Really." Lady Nightmare straightened her hat and cleared her throat. "So...uh, would you maybe want to get a cup of coffee sometime, or.... No." She glanced around. "I broke into your apartment and psy-assaulted you. This isn't appropriate timing, is it? Shit. Um."

If Sara had been flying, now she dropped like a rock. So she wasn't getting asked out, then?

"Hold on. Here." Lady Nightmare walked over to the kitchen table, picked up a pen, and scribbled something on one of the unopened envelopes piled there. Then she handed the envelope to Sara. There was a phone number scribbled on it.

"Take a few weeks to yourself, get some space," Lady Nightmare said, "Then, if you're still interested, give me a call. No pressure."

Sara smiled for what felt like the first time in days. "I will."

"You don't have to. I don't want you to feel obligated—"

"I'll talk to you in a few weeks," Sara said firmly.

Lady Nightmare made another call on her cell, and a minute later, a muscled minion came to drag Captain Alpha out of the apartment. Sara walked Lady Nightmare to the door like a polite hostess, never mind that she hadn't intended to host anything.

Lady Nightmare stopped outside the threshold. "I'm Bianca, by the way. Bianca Belmonte."

"Sara Jovanovic."

Sara, feeling daring, went in for a hug goodbye at the exact moment Lady Nightmare stuck out her hand for a handshake. After an awkward pause, Lady Nightmare—no, *Bianca* kissed her on the cheek and walked away with a bounce in her step.

Sara closed the door and sighed contentedly. She would have to call the police in ten minutes, but at least she had a date to look forward to after. And the next time Bianca came over, Sara would make sure to clean her apartment beforehand. The two of them might hit it off, or they might not, but it would be fun to find out either way.

No matter what happened, it would definitely be better than her last date.

Rose Briar, Briar Rose

Miranda Schmidt

Miranda Schmidt's work has appeared or is forthcoming in The Collagist, Phoebe, Driftwood Press, and other journals. Miranda grew up in the Midwest and now lives with her partner and two cats in Portland, Oregon where she edits the Sun Star Review, teaches at Portland Community College and occasionally blogs about books at mirandaschmidt.com. A graduate of the University of Washington's MFA program, Miranda recently completed a novel about haunting and is currently at work on a project inspired by shapeshifting fairy tales.

It is the rose that people see: the lovely lips, the soft gold hair, the long lashed eyes gone pale and closed in sleeping. They think, those who think to try to brave them, that the briars are just plant life, separate things grown over and around the woman at their center. They do not see that the briars, too, are hers. The briars spin themselves from dreams. They are the world behind her face, grown real and full of thorns.

She lies completely still. Some of the knights think her dead, she is so pale. But the pale in her skin makes her lips look more red, so they say, makes her lips look like rose petals, makes her lashes as dark as the raven. She is vaguely aware of the men that tromp by her, of their footsteps that echo on the empty stone stairs, of the ways that they whisper, voices gone soft in the silence that reigns in her castle.

All the knights are the same, hacking their way through the mazes of thorns until, finally, they all reach her bed. Each one stops, every time, to gaze down at her beauty. They are momentarily frozen by the frozenness of her. But soon they recover and they bend towards her lips and they kiss them gently at first, timid and shy, guilty perhaps, just a little, at kissing a stranger who's sleeping. And once they kiss they wait, watching for her eyes to burst open and look upon them with fear or confusion or love.

When her eyes do not open, they kiss her again, harder this time, and with passion, as if their lips must convince her to wake.

They wait and some, seeing no stirring, walk away, leave her dreaming just as they'd found her. Some try kissing yet harder and longer. Some kiss with increasing frustration until they are shouting into her silence, calling her to wake, wake, wake, wake up. But she never does. And, eventually, even the most stubborn man leaves, taking his vine-cutting sword and his echoing boots back out of the castle in failure.

On their way out they must step over, of course, all the servants, both the king and the queen, the cooks and the housekeepers, the nobles and jesters, all slumped on the floor, fallen sleep-ward when she did, that one time, long ago, when she pricked her finger on the needle of a spinning wheel they told her not to touch. The wheel, she knew, was magicked, the needle cursed to make her what she was, to bring the inside out, the outside in, flipped world-ward and dreaming, exposed in her sleep. She did it on purpose, the pricking. She was tired, so tired, of the way they kept hiding the spinning. She was sick of the sharp prick of fear that she felt when she saw the flashing of points in the lamplight, of how conscious she was, always and forever, that one misplaced finger could drive her to change. So she reached out her finger one night, just the tip, and touched it deliberately, pushed her flesh to its point until it broke through her skin and drew blood and, after that, she felt only the dreaming.

It is not a bad thing, this sleep. In fact, she prefers it to the fuss of before, to the hiding away with three fairies in the forest, to the dreading, always, the wickedness of witches, and the fear, forever the fear, of being turned inside out without warning. Because she's felt them inside, the vines and the briars, the needle-like thorns, felt them growing, expanding, pushing forward just under her skin. She's felt them as long she's felt anything. And it is a relief, she thinks, now, to have them out on the surface, even if it means the entire castle is sleeping, gone silent beneath all her vining.

It is finally a woman who wakes her, not a knight but a gardener. She does not bend towards her lips like the others. Instead she bends to the briars that grow up around them. She kisses each thorn, one by one, until her eyelids flutter open and she gazes, still half dreaming, upon her and thinks that, perhaps, this woman has found her, discovered the secret-est part of herself and embraced it with love. She looks at her, not with the horror she thinks she expected, but with something else, with a thing that seems like admiration. When she kisses her lips, she is still half sleeping, half inside, half outside, her dreams.

The gardener lies down beside her, burrowing into her vines, and she closes her eyes as if she, too, is sleeping. She does not know how long they lie together, two closed-eyed strangers, on a bed hidden underneath thorns.

When she fully wakes, as she must, she is more plant than human, outside as well as in. Now it shows on her face, the hint of green, the tendril curve of vine-like veining—not enough so they know, not for sure. The sleeping castle wakes with relief. The king and the queen, the cooks and the housekeepers, the nobles and jesters are shocked when they find out their savior is not a noble knight, not a prince, but a simple gardener—and a woman one at that. But who are they to argue with magic? True love's kiss has won them back their waking so they celebrate the end of the curse, the beginning of their princess's marriage. They do not remark on the way she seems faded, worn down, less rose-like than she seemed before.

It has been, they realize, centuries since the sleeping began. They have all, they think graciously, aged somewhat, even if her aging looks different, unsettling in a way none can name. Even if her once blue eyes (they were blue once, weren't they?) have gone green and her once soft full hair (it was soft before, wasn't it?) has gone wiry, her lips are still the deep red of roses.

But her gardener still thinks her beautiful, inhumanly so. She says so sometimes when they lie in bed at night before sleeping, when she gazes down at her with that thing that must be love glowing out of her eyes.

"Yours," she says then, "is a beauty grown out from inside." She says it with pride as if the words should please her.

She is not, she thinks, displeased, though she longs sometimes, as they lay side by side in a bed made of cushions and blankets and pillows and all the soft things that their castle provides, for her bed made of briars, for her dreams vining out of her, surrounding her, surrounding them, surrounding the castle: a fortress, a burrow, a maze made of silence where not even leaves dared to rustle.

...But Not Too Bold

L.M. Davenport

L.M. Davenport has read Ursula
K. Le Guin's The Left Hand of
Darkness a ridiculous number of
times, and once knitted a five-and-
a-half-foot-long giant squid. Her
work has previously appeared at
Hobart and Shimmer.

In the chair to the left of the stove, in the first room of the house under the copse of bare trees at the end of the road, sat the house-holder's friend. She was still wearing her coat and hat, but she had pulled her arms out of the sleeves so that they dangled vacant at her sides, and stuck both limbs through the open front to hold an enormous mug of very bitter tea. She gulped at the hot liquid, winced, and torqued her head around to crane at the stove.

"Renard," she said in a high voice that tripped over itself in her throat, "is there anything else I can do?"

The house-holder, who was kneeling in front of the open stove, feeding it scraps of wood and wads of newspaper, shook his head. Renard was not his name, but it was what she called him. He did not call her anything.

She turned again to the tea, blowing on its surface this time before drinking. Renard sat back on his heels, with his eyes closed and face turned towards the belly of the stove. Outside, the sound of the wind grew deeper and more insistent. A branch scraped against the side window, like the fingernails of a bad witch. A draft nosed through a cracked windowpane, whispered against her face. She put both sock feet on the warped wooden floor, felt that it was cold from the other draft coming in under the door. She had never liked the cold. She picked her feet back up.

The branch moved again, rapid-fire jittering scratches this time.

Like the fractured rhythm Renard's first three fingers tapped out on his thigh. Neither of them spoke.

The room warmed and she shed her coat, sitting in jeans and a men's flannel shirt with her knees drawn up against her chest. Every time she breathed, she was afraid that the motion of her body would crack the chair, rupture the house walls, leave them both exposed to the indifferent night.

She wondered if he wanted her to go. It was very late. Renard said, without opening his eyes, "I'm sorry there wasn't any sugar. Are you still cold?"

"That's all right. And no. Thank you for building the fire—I never learned how." She shifted in her chair, feeling the coldness and the lateness of the night more clearly than she had when they had been walking in it. (Had it been a day already, was this the second night?)

"Ah, yes." His eyes were still closed. He brushed a forefinger across the bandage wrapped neatly around his left wrist.

This was the way that she had seem him reach, so many times, for the spines of the paperbacks stacked and scattered around the room, the mug she still gripped with both hands, the bright soiled wool of a blanket. Directed at himself, it was a touch as blind as his shuttered eyes.

"That's okay," she said, and wondered immediately why she had said it. It was not okay. She remembered the road, lime gravel washed white as paper by the full moon, and the blood that would have been livid in daylight but with her human night vision looked like innocent splotches of ink. And the long silent minutes in the second room when Renard held out his wrist like a child with a skinned knee and she wrapped it and gave wordless thanks that he had not thought of the proper direction to cut. The moon was not full tonight; it would not be full again for weeks.

He said only, "Feed the stove with me." She left her coat slumped in a pile on the chair, and sat on the floor. Renard opened the stove door and handed her a narrow strip of wood, which she tentatively poked inside. They did not touch.

Then, softly: "Tell me a story."

"Once," she said, "there was a little house in the middle of a deep dark forest, at the end of a white road." She took a crumpled twist of newspaper from the floor and tossed it into the stove. "In the summer," she continued, wishing that her voice weren't quite so high, "the house and its road were almost hidden by the great old trees that arched over them like a second house, and by the spreading vines with narrow, sharp-tipped leaves and small white flowers. When the winter came, everything around the house was stark and bare, and then people had reason to shun the road that shone as pure as the blossoms of the vine, for they could see what the greenery had concealed from them—that it was Death's house." Then she flushed. Silence would have been better. She glanced at Renard out of the corner of her eye, and saw that his eyes were closed again and that he was hunched forward, listening. With the ruddy light on his face and hands, he was the most fragile thing that she had ever seen.

"Enough," Renard said, stretching and opening his eyes. "The story is over, and now it is time to get into the stove." He leaned towards the mouth of the woodstove, sliding his hands in first, as though he were parting branches in a jungle. She did not move or cry out, because it seemed, at this hour, in this place, that it was time to get into the stove. (She had almost forgotten that there was a house around them by now, and the legs of the table beside her, if she had cared to look at them, were like the bare trees out-side that reached up into fathomless darkness.) At first, she didn't think that Renard would fit, but either the stove seemed to grow bigger or he seemed to become smaller, and very soon he had gotten inside without any difficulty at all.

"Come on," he called out in a voice that echoed oddly against the iron, sounding nearly as tinny as her own.

"I can't," she cried back. She knew that she could, but also that she was afraid.

Still Renard beckoned to her, smiling. Flames danced around his feet, and his whole body looked no taller than her hand. And, the longer she peered into the stove, with her face so close it nearly pressed into the edges of the opening, the easier it seemed. So she, too, stretched out her hands, and found that they fit through the door, and that she was not burned. She put her head inside, and though it was warm (so warm that her lips felt dry, and she had to stop herself from licking them), she still did not burn. And, before she knew it, she was inside the stove.

She turned to Renard, who was standing ankle-deep in a mass of coals with his arms thrown wide and his head flung back, star-ing up the long narrow tunnel of the stove-pipe. Around them, the iron walls curved up and closed in like the walls of a cave, and there was a slight, pleasant taste of smoke in the hazy, red-lit air. The coals underfoot were the texture of loose gravel, and the great chunks of wood with fire streaming from their tops and flickering along their sides jutted upwards like the remains of a sunken ship.

She had not closed the door behind her when she came in, and because it still hung open she went to the edge of the stove and looked out. Though she did not turn around, she heard Renard's footsteps, and knew that he had come to stand behind her. The house, the whole world beyond the stove, seemed so impossibly enormous to her now that she wondered how she could ever have fit into it. The wind, the tapping branch, the waning moon that still bleached the gravel road, all felt as though someone else had heard and seen and walked over them. As she thought this, she was struck by the desire just to touch the air that she had so recently breathed. Before Renard could move to stop her, she had put one finger, the first finger of her right hand, out of the stove.

It shriveled into ash so quickly that it looked as if a knife had severed her finger at the knuckle. She did not bleed, and when she jerked her hand back to examine the wound, there was only a shining red scar, as red as the coals beneath her feet. She stared at it, not willing to think hard about what it meant, and jumped, startled, when Renard laid a hand on her shoulder and said "Come on" again, more softly. She allowed him to lead her to the very back of the stove, skirting the places where the fire was already starting to die down.

They slithered in between the great logs, Renard first and her after, and burrowed into the bed of coals together until they were completely buried, and lay curled as one creature against the iron. And there they waited, at the heart of this inmost, bloodless chamber of the house.

Morning, and it seemed to her that, although they had not left the stove, the world outside had reassembled itself around them. That they lay, not upon iron, but loose white gravel. Above, when she gathered the courage to lift her head, stretched a sky very nearly the same color as the road. She blinked several times, sniffed the air for traces of smoke, disentangled herself from the still-sleeping Renard and sat up. It was impossible to tell the time; though the curtained sun hung at an angle, she had never in her life been able to make out which way was north. She tilted her head back, craning up at the leafless branches.

Renard knew all the trees, even in winter. He had tried to teach her once, but the only one she could still recognize in all seasons was the poplar, from the way its branches curled in wavefronts out of a straight trunk like a mast. She had felt guilty about this, until the day six months before when she had gone to Renard's house for tea and he had brought it to her unsweetened, with milk.

"Isn't that the way you like it?" he asked, when she took a sip and grimaced involuntarily. He looked so sure, wearing that expansive, hungry smile that cut his face open like a wound. She could have told him the truth, or simply reached for the crumpled bag of sugar that sat on the countertop behind her. But either of those actions would have closed up the smile and restored Renard to normal, the bright eyes and grave, still features that had sliced her to the bone the first time she saw them, and still did when she wasn't careful. With his teeth showing, he couldn't hurt her.

After a while, she wasn't certain of how she had liked her tea in the first place.

Now, standing in the road, she looked down at Renard and saw that his bandage was missing, the skin whole and unscarred. Startled, she turned to her own right hand, which now had five fingers again, instead of four. But, on inspection, her left leg was still slightly shorter than her right, and both knees still bore the mottled scars of her early attempts to ride a bicycle. And, when she checked Renard's hands, her touch tentative and delicate, she found that the many tiny marks of his own life—oil burns, nicks off of kitchen knives, a still-unhealed scrape from a branch or a jagged rock—remained.

But this felt too much like something a lover would do. She released his hands and turned away.

And then she saw that Renard's eyes were slitted open and that he was waiting, limp, to see what she would do next. How long had he been awake, and watching her?

"I'm going," she said, startled by the sound of the words made as they came out of her mouth. She turned, intending to follow the road back to its origin, back to the world, and Renard watched but did not stop her. She walked along the curves of the road as it slid between the pines, twisting and turning until Renard was out of sight. As she went, she tried to remember that she had had a life beyond him and his strange, drafty house, a life with other people in it, and work, and a stove with grease-encrusted coils that glowed a brilliant, sick tomato-red but never held fire. But all that she could see as she walked were the places on the road that had been stained with his blood.

She paused and looked up. It was fully dark now, though she still could not tell in what direction the road led. The clouds were dissolving, and the moon was rising.

The moon was full.

She knew, then. Even so, it was not until she rounded the next curve and saw Renard waiting for her in a shaft of cold light that she allowed herself to fully understand.

This time, it was she who put out a hand, and Renard who came forward to take it. When they met, her hand had only four fingers once again. There was blood sliding down his wrist, and when it met their joined hands she tightened her grip. Together they walked back towards the house, leaving a red trail between them, as they pursued the dying fire for this and every other night.

All Better Now

Casey Cooke

Casey Cooke writes speculative
fiction and horror, and her work
has been published in a variety of
literary magazines. In addition to
writing, she works as an adjunct
instructor.

Astrid's power sensor beeped. Her systems were functioning, but with less than thirty percent power remaining, her biological enhancements were losing shape. All of the angles in her face, made to create a Kusuvian illusion, were softening. Not that it mattered. They were done for the sake of the crew, who were now all in stasis, and for the rest of the Kusuvians they'd meet at the space station.

She pulled up the ship's schematics, looking for power reserves. Over the last few months, she'd shut off the observation deck, mess, and gym. Now, she decided on the aeroponics bay. The life support in that section clicked off. It was the last nonessential system.

Two tubules spiraled out of her wrist and plugged themselves into the closest bioport. While she waited for them to pull power, she scanned the spatial void. There was a flash of light. An anomaly? She scanned again. No. Sensor malfunction. There wasn't anything out here. The void's end was still a parsec away.

"I hate the dark," she muttered.

She should have been fully charged by now, but she hovered at fifty percent. She retracted her biomechanical veins and left for the engineering compartment. She watched the engine turn, pumping electricity into wires and liquid quinite into tubes. She pushed her palm against a tube, testing the quinite's flow rate. It flowed steadily and pushed back against her with a subtle rhythm: Th-thud. Th-thud.

"Biomechanical ships do not have heartbeats," she chastised. "You're not supposed to start and stop. The flow should be constant. Now, where is the malfunction coming from?"

She pulled her hand away to investigate, but as she searched the engine, she still felt it: Th-thud. Th-thud. She looked down to her wrist and watched, frozen, as a vein pulsed just beneath the synthaskin.

It's coming from me.

She reeled. Malfunction. It's a malfunction. Her vision matrix was off, simulated breathing erratic. The synthaskin over her cheeks and neck overheated. There was ringing in her ears. Suddenly, she realized these weren't symptoms of a malfunction. "Fear," she said, breathless. "This is fear. When did they program me to feel fear?"

"I fixed you." A small girl appeared beside her, smiling.

Normally, Astrid would have alerted the ship to an intruder, but she was overwhelmed as she tried to analyze her systems. She struggled to focus. "You fixed me?"

"You were missing all your squishy stuff. You're all better now."

Astrid leaned over. "Is that why I'm..." she groaned, "sick to my stomach?"

"I didn't know how many you wanted. I had three once and hated it. But I liked having two. Do you? Most of your crew had two, too, so I thought you'd like that best."

Astrid grimaced. "No... Oh. OH. What's that smell?"

"Kusivian stress pheremones, I'm guessing."

"You had no right," Astrid turned in a slow circle, searching for a spot to focus on. She pulled at the skin on the sides of her stomach; she felt the scent glands underneath her ribs and moaned.

She started to sob and brought a horrified hand up to her cheek, then she held out her hand to the girl. "I was perfect. Now look at me. I'm leaking!"

"Tears," the girl offered cooly.

"I know what they are," Astrid said, sullen. She felt the spines along her nose. "You could have at least made me Benithai. Or Rhodisi."

"But your face is too fat."

"Really?" Astrid marched up to her, seething. "You can give me two stomachs and glands, but you can't make my face less FAT?"

"I could I guess, but I like your fat face."

Astrid threw a punch, but missed and hit the engine. "Ow. Oh, ow. Pain? Pain... this is awful... I think I broke my hand."

"You should get that looked at."

Astrid opened her mouth, but a beeping noise stopped her. "What's that?" she asked, still seething, "Kusivian tympanic disruption? Because I'm not defective enough now? You know they're going to decommission me when they wake up. I'm useless now."

"You're so melodramatic." The girl laughed. "That, silly robot, is your stasis pod."

***

Astrid was awake, still lying down in her stasis pod. As her internal sensors clicked back on, she noticed something unusual. As the crewman helped her out of her pod, she asked, "did the doctor equip me with dreaming protocols? I have... an unusual log entry in my data banks."

The doctor came over from across the room. "I bet you do," he said. "Your power was completely drained; you know what kind of data corruption that can cause. We shouldn't have left you alone so long. When the sensors picked up the planet, and we woke up, you were on the floor. You managed to crack your head pretty good, too."

"So you put me in stasis?"

He nodded. "Your skin hasn't healed yet, though. It's kind of gruesome." He handed her a small mirror, so she could assess the damage. There was a deep gash, exposing her upper cranial plate.

Astrid reached up with her free hand and peeled off the rest of the synthaskin, exposing her metal plating. All traces of Kusuvi were gone. "Is that better?" she asked.

He shrugged. "It's something, that's for sure."

Slowly, she started peeling the skin from her arms and chest. Then, once they'd left the room, she pulled it off the rest of her frame. When she was finished, it lay in a crumpled damp pile on the floor. She looked at herself in the mirror again. She panned it up and down her body, noticing how her frame glinted underneath the fluorescent lights, and how all of her softness was gone. She ran a hand along her torso; her sensors indicated that just beneath was a perfectly ordered collection of wires and tubes. Her metallic metatarsals curved onto the floor like talons.

There, she thought, smiling. All better.

Genie's Retirement

Sarah Newman

Sarah Newman writes TV pilots, screenplays, and short fiction. She lives in New York City.

You can find Sarah chatting about writing as @SarahAlexis4 on Twitter and posting writing-related photos (that showcase her notebook addiction) as @WriteCreateBe on Instagram.

I watched Genie with great admiration and love as she whipped up our pancake breakfast. She had a perfectly symmetrical face, a sturdy jawline, kind eyes, and a perpetual soft smile. Her lustrous brown hair was always tucked neatly into an impeccable bun.

Genie was part of our family for as long as I remember. When I was a baby she was the only one who could get me to stop fussing. My parents said she had the magic touch. She always had a way of soothing me when I'd get hurt, whether it was a scraped knee, a stomach ache, or a heavy heart.

"Can you make heart shapes today?" I said, picking at the sliced banana and blueberries on my plate. Genie made me eat fruit or I wouldn't get my pancakes. It was our deal.

"Of course, my little Olive," she said.

It made my heart swell when Genie called me that. The nickname stuck even after I turned four and learned my name was actually Olivia.

"Your appointment was rescheduled for one, Ella," Genie said. She handed mom her coffee, prepared just the way she liked it.

"Thanks, Genie," mom said, quickly taking a sip as she scrolled through emails projected by her watch onto the surface of the table.

Dad ambled in with his tie loose around his neck. He stood next to Genie and waited as she poured batter on the griddle. She turned to him and tied his necktie in a perfect Windsor knot.

My brother Caleb coasted in on his hoverboard.

"What did I tell you about riding that in the house?" Mom said.

Genie playfully ruffled Caleb's hair as he tried to steal a pancake. She was the only one allowed to touch his hair without receiving his teenage attitude.

"You have the dentist after baseball, Caleb." Genie leaned in closer and used her hushed voice, though it wasn't as hushed as she thought. "I found some personal items while cleaning your room. I put them in your sock drawer."

Caleb smiled devilishly and gave Genie a high five. "You're the best, G."

"Here's your permission slip, my little Olive."

"Thanks," I said, shoving the paper into my backpack. I totally forgot about that.

"Breakfast is almost ready," Genie said.

Dad and Caleb joined me and Mom at the table.

Our kitchen was equipped with the latest gadgets, but Genie kept things a bit old school. It took a little longer, but we didn't mind. She flipped pancakes with such flare. A big smile spread across her face.

There wasn't a single wrinkle on Genie's face. Even though she was getting on in years. She always looked the same. It was comforting actually. Genie was an early Genesis Model. A household AI robot. When I was little I didn't understand what that meant. To me, Genie was as real and human as we were. But it started to become clear that Genie was a machine. And she was indeed aging.

***

It started with little things. Genie was helping me with home-work. She tried to show me a math equation with her built-in projection system. But the image kept flickering, dancing across my teal bedroom wall. I figured she just needed a replacement lamp or a lens cleaning.

One day when Dad came home late and the rest of us were asleep, I woke to him scolding Genie for not properly securing the house. I guess she hadn't interfaced with the security system to lock up and activate the alarm. Dad rarely got cross with her like that. I pulled my blanket over my head but was unable to stop my tears.

Genie was an amazing cook. She had access to every recipe book imaginable. I could tell she had fun in the kitchen. But that energy faded away. The food started tasting off, like she used a wrong ingredient or left some out. We all noticed but nobody wanted to say anything. I believed she had feelings, even if she wasn't made to. She always sat with us for family meals though she didn't eat. So we ate the food and smiled at Genie.

I noticed Genie wasn't as quick as she used to be. She used to glide around and move with such efficiency. Her hands developed slight tremors. She could no longer give Dad a hot shave, or catch Caleb's pitches, or paint Mom's nails, or color in the lines when we did art projects.

***

I sat with Genie in the back of our car. She nervously gazed out the window. I didn't blame her. I didn't like going to the doctor either. Dad sat up front reading on his tablet while the car drove us.

"I spy with my little eye something green," I said, trying to take Genie's processor off the situation. We played until the car came to a stop in front of a repair shop with signs that read "Parts and Maintenance" and "We repair all robot models."

A scrawny guy in a work shirt and oil smeared jeans gave Genie a once over and hooked her up to a diagnostic program. I didn't like the way he rubbed the scruff on his chin as he said, "To be honest, sir, it ain't worth it."

"She's not an 'it,' her name is Genie," I said. He smirked at me, indifferent.

Dad handed me a credit card and nudged me to a flashy vending machine that sold all kinds of goodies. He nodded to Genie to accompany me. I took Genie's hand and we shuffled over. Normally I'd be deeply invested in what to get from this delightful machine but we could still hear the guy.

"You're gonna sink a buttload of money into repairs that won't make much difference. Don't even know if we could get the parts. Might as well just get a new model."

I squeezed Genie's hand tighter and she squeezed back two quick squeezes. That was our thing. Two quick squeezes meant it's all going to be okay.

It was a quiet and tense drive back home.

***

Within a week our new household AI robot arrived. I passionately spoke out against this at our family meeting but my parents assured me Genie would remain with us.

Neko was sleek and had many features Genie didn't. But I didn't care. We were all standoffish at first. Neko was likable. She just wasn't Genie.

Genie followed Neko around and told her how she was doing everything wrong. She didn't appreciate Neko messing up her methods for completing chores and changing the way the household was run. Neko tried to be patient but they were both insistent on their own way. Nothing was getting done with them undermining each other.

Mom and Dad deactivated some of Genie's settings so Neko was solely responsible for running the house. They were quickly won over by Neko's efficiency. Caleb's allegiance was earned with some younger model robot cleavage.

Genie became more like an old senile grandma, sitting there smiling but not fully there. Taking away her purpose aged her even more.

I still cherished our time together. I'd read her stories and some nights we'd sleep under a blanket tent I made. This could work I thought. Genie could be retired and still be part of the family. But soon we discovered that couldn't be.

***

I was the only human home when it happened. Neko was in the basement doing laundry. Genie sat with me in the kitchen as I struggled to do my homework.

"I would like to reward you for your good effort, my little Olive," she said. "Would you like some fresh baked cookies?"

I nodded vigorously. Genie got to work, humming as she prepared the ingredients.

I was in my room putting pajamas on when the smoke detectors went off. I rushed downstairs.

Smoke and flames shot up from the stove where a potholder caught fire next to a burning pan of caramel sauce.

Genie paced, fretting and wringing her hands. "I left it too long. I forgot."

Neko rushed in. She grabbed the fire extinguisher and tamed the flames.

Mom and Dad weren't happy to see the kitchen when they got home. But more than that they were scared for our safety.

***

I was surprised when a week later, with the kitchen restored, my parents invited Genie to make pancake breakfast for us.

"Genie, would you like to join us on an outing to the beach?" Dad said. It was as if he were forcing a cheery disposition. I could see a sadness in his eyes.

"We know it's your favorite place to go," Mom added.

"But being by seawater isn't good for her internal rusting," I said.

Mom looked at me with a gentle smile. "It's okay. Today will be a fun day with no worries."

I had a feeling something was up but I didn't want to believe there were other motives, like guilt, behind my parents' plan.

That night after the beach the five of us sat in front of the projection wall in the living room and watched old family videos. Genie cheering me on as she captured my first steps, Genie preparing the first solid food mom fed me, Genie teaching me my ABCs, birthday parties, first days of school, all the milestones in my life with Genie there. Genie appeared to be bursting with pride as she watched. I think if she could have, she would have cried.

***

The next morning Dad had us all pile into the car. I thought perhaps we were going on another family outing. We were. Just not the kind I imagined.

Mom and Dad were quiet up front. I sat next to Genie and noticed her face drop. I followed her gaze to the car's navigation screen with the address for "Robot Retirement Facility" as the destination. Genie sat quietly resigned. I clenched my fists as my heart was pounding out of my chest.

The car stopped in front of the building.

"We're so sorry, Genie, but we think it's time," Dad blurted.

Mom could barely look at her. "You know we love—"

"I understand," Genie said. "I want the family to be safe and happy."

"No!" I said. "You can't do this."

Dad dragged me kicking and screaming.

***

The inside of the retirement facility was drab and industrial. There was an area full of all different robot models that were powered down. They looked creepy. Especially the ones whose eyes were still open. There was another area in the back where they were being dismantled for parts for refurbishment. Something I'd later have nightmares of.

I saw Genie's eyes flick around, taking this all in, taking in her fate. I wondered if she was scared.

A middle-aged woman came over and ushered us to a private room where we could say goodbye and witness Genie's shutdown.

It was clean and bright. Soft classical music played. My parents shared their gratitude and said goodbye. I knew they genuinely meant it but I rolled my eyes at them for this betrayal. I noticed Caleb tearing up. He never cried. He and Genie did their secret handshake and he gave her a quick hug.

I stepped up to Genie and buried myself in her chest. "I'll never forget you."

"I know, my little Olive. I'll always be with you."

Genie lied down on a cold metal table. The woman plugged a USB cord into the control panel on Genie's side. She strapped Genie's arms and legs down.

Through tears I pleaded, "Please don't do that."

"I'm afraid it's a safety precaution," the woman said. "Sometimes there are involuntary reactions during system shutdown."

I moved closer to Genie and held her hand. Genie squeezed two quick squeezes.

The woman began the shutdown process. I watched as the life

drained from Genie. She was more real than ever to me in that moment. And then she was gone. Her hand went limp in mine.

As we left the building the woman handed me a small box. "I think she would want you to have this. Her heart and soul."

Inside was a computer chip. I picked it up, closed my hand around it, and gave it two quick squeezes.

Sex After Fascism

Audie Shushan

Audie Shushan lives in Chicago, IL, where she teaches English for the City Colleges. She holds a BA from the University of Michigan and an MFA from the University of Washington, where she was the recipient of the 2014 Eugene Van Buren Prize for Fiction. Her work has appeared in Sun Star Review.

Daryl and I are driving to Chicago's Midway Airport, for unknown reasons.

Well–not unknown, probably. Just untold to me.

Daryl called me at midnight, told me to pack a bag for two days, he'd be at my house in half an hour, and I should come out and meet him. He's my boss–as in, I work for him. Also, I love him. Which isn't kosher, exactly, but it's a temporary job. And a temporary love.

It's October, and I can't figure out what to pack, so I leaf through the fashion magazines my roommate keeps stacked on our coffee table. The glossy models counsel me to be both realistic and idealistic. Dress for the job you want, not the job you have, one advises me. On the next page they tell me to rein myself in, to dress for the body I have, not the body I want. I have neither the job I want nor the body I'd like, so I take both pieces of wisdom and decide to dress for the weather I want, not the weather I have.

I pack summer clothes and put on a tank top and a striped skirt. No jacket. I leave a note on the table for my roommate and go downstairs to wait for Daryl. On the street, the wind blows my skirt up, causing a pack of drunken boys driving by to wolf whistle at me. My vain optimism has (again) left me exposed and shivering. I remind myself of those other sage pieces of advice, the kind that people carve into driftwood and hang on their walls, to dance like nobody's watching, and love like I've never been hurt. I decide that what I'm doing is brave. I am dressing like I've never been cold.

Thankfully, Daryl pulls up the next minute, rolling down the window of his shiny sedan and telling me to get in because I look freezing.

I throw my bag in the backseat and turn the heat up full blast.

On our way out of the city, we hit a red light beneath the underpass for I-90. Overhead, the highways are a rush of noise, a river of lights. This late at night, the headlights look less like the eyes of predators and more like the beams from a lighthouse, calling the ships home.

The city is dimly lit, always, even in the middle of the day, even in the middle of the night. A man walks slowly along the length of stopped cars. Over his shoulder is a rod the length of a vaulting pole, which he carries like a runaway child might carry his rucksack. Bags of pink and blue cotton candy dangle from the pole, spaced evenly along the length of it.

"You think anyone actually buys that stuff?" I ask Daryl.

"What I want to know is, where's this guy getting cotton candy?" he says.

"Like, is it organically sourced?" I say, cracking myself up.

Daryl doesn't laugh. "Yes," he says, turning to stare at me. His eyes are so blue I feel like drowning. "Exactly."

I can't decide whether to laugh or match his stare, so I compromise and choke a little on the spit gathering under my tongue.

How could I not fall in love with a man who does that to me?

***

The first time I met Daryl, he swept me off my feet.

I mean, he picked me up.

It's not an easy thing to do—men hardly ever try. I'm 5'11" and I have the wingspan of a sandhill crane. Which is six feet and some change, if you're wondering.

I was standing in the middle of the office—Daryl's office—and I'd gotten myself stuck. What I mean is, I couldn't move. And not for any good reason, like quicksand, or a net trap, or anything. It was my first day on the job and my first month being single and I was in the middle of the plush green carpet, in the waiting area of the law office, about a foot from the gleaming wood desk where I would be answering phones and greeting clients, and my legs had stopped working of their own accord. I couldn't move at all.

Daryl swooped in, like some oversize bird himself, and plucked me up, right off the carpet. He twirled me around and I felt the world grow larger and larger.

"Welcome to the firm," he said, and his voice was like milk warmed on the stove. Creamy. Sweet.

I swayed on the new spot he'd placed me in and felt laughter bubble up in me.

But this wasn't the moment I fell in love with Daryl.

I fell in love with Daryl because he brought me pie in the middle of the night when I couldn't sleep.

It was rhubarb, which, as everyone knows, is the best kind of pie.

I would have fallen in love with him even if he'd brought me a terrible kind of pie, though—like pecan. Or mincemeat.

Because he took me to see his friend's bluegrass band, and when I asked if people were going to dance, he took my beer away from me and led me up to the stage, where we danced alone to a cover of an old Bob Dylan song on dark carpet with ground-in popcorn kernels and an inexplicable disco ball twirled above our heads.

I fell in love with Daryl, because when he found me trying to make his bed, nearly in tears because the blankets wouldn't fit right, he didn't say anything, just took the blankets away from me and said, let's sit down for a minute.

He put his arms around me and held me while I cried, there on his imperfectly made bed, at six in the morning.

My ex-boyfriend, Tony, once told me that my emotions were like a badly trained St. Bernard: too messy, too slobbery, and too big for their own good. He thought this was quite a clever and poetic thing to say.

You can see why he's an ex.

***

At the airport, Daryl walks quickly and with purpose to our gate. I keep asking him where we're going, and he keeps grinning at me like a little kid.

I find this unbearably endearing.

The gate says Kalamazoo, MI, but there's no one there. Daryl pulls me forward. "Hurry," he says.

The door to the jetway is open for some reason, and we can see the plane outside, so we board ourselves.

The plane is tiny, a little toy of a thing, with two seats on each side of the aisle and no more than eight rows. There's a man in a suit dozing against one of the windows and a flight attendant who smiles cheerily at us.

"You just made it!" she says. "Sit down, sit down. It doesn't matter where."

I seatbelt myself in and press my face to the window and then we're airborne. Below us, the dim city fades into dim suburbia fades into dim nothingness. I glance over at Daryl. He's reading–he's always reading–and tonight he has a book called, mysteriously, Sex After Fascism. Stalin is featured on the cover.

In many ways, I know I'm a cliché. The secretary and her lawyer boss. A cliché, or a porno flick. But I also know something that Daryl doesn't. That I'm falling in love, not with him, but with my own life. There is so much possibility in the world. This is a temporary job and a temporary love and my hands are on the walls of my world and I am pushing outwards.

The plane begins to descend. It's almost dawn now, and the sky is lightening. As we near the ground, the sandhill cranes come into view. Hundreds and hundreds of them, clustered together on the browning grass, so that it's difficult to pick one out from the others. They blur together in a great red and brown cloud.

Daryl's still reading. I glance over his shoulder: he's on a chapter entitled "Toledo." The word on the page makes my heart jolt, and I press my face back against the cool glass of the window, watching the cranes.

A year ago, I lived in a small suburb of Toledo, in western Ohio. That summer, Lake Erie bloomed with algae. It carried a toxin that couldn't be killed. Boiling the water only made it stronger, more concentrated. We were advised not to use any water at all and all the restaurants and shops shut down for the summer.

I used the water anyway.

The day they announced that the water was toxic and we shouldn't touch it, Tony didn't come home until past midnight.

I kept my phone next to me all night, though in my heart I knew he wouldn't call. Tony was busy, he had work, he had friends, he didn't need to check in and he didn't need me to act like his mother. I let him tell me all of this each night and still, I'd made dinner: salmon and asparagus and rice, all cooked with the water, before I knew it was toxic.

I waited until ten, until the rice was hard and the asparagus was cold and the salmon was congealed, and then I shut my phone in the bathroom and went outside to eat by myself. There was no one else out; even the streetlamps seemed dimmer. I felt I might be the only person left in the world.

When I came back inside, Tony still wasn't home. My phone watched me silently. I'd left the TV on, and the bleached blonde newscaster was telling the residents of Toledo to absolutely not use the water. Below her, the words "Water Warning!" flashed in yellow.

I filled a bowl with warm tap water and scrubbed down the whole apartment.

When Tony finally came home, I was already in bed, though I'd left all the lights on. I could hear him in the living room; there was a sharp thump! and he cursed and then he was in the doorway of the bedroom.

"How was your day?" I said.

"Terrible."

"Oh. I'm sorry," I said. I was always sorry. "How come you're home so late?"

"I was working," he said, and his voice was surly.

"You could've called," I said.

"Sorry," he said. He was always sorry, too.

I rolled over onto my side. "I was worried," I said. "I made dinner."

"Kris, I'm under a lot of pressure at work right now. You have no idea. I've barely been sleeping."

"I know," I said. "I share a bed with you."

"Fucking Sandy at work can't get anything right. I have to do everything."

"Oh," I said.

"She's such a cunt. And disgusting. Today she was talking about dieting and then she went out to lunch and brought back fries and I had to watch her stuff them all in her fat fucking mouth."

I was curled up and I could feel the rolls of skin and fat on my own stomach.

"That's a shitty thing to say," I said.

"Well, she's a shitty person."

"I really wish you would've called."

"Fine," he said. "Fine. You win. I'm selfish and mean and a terrible person."

"Well," I said. "Not always."

I tried to make it a joke, but we could both hear that it wasn't. Tony went into the living room and slammed the bedroom door shut, turning off the light as he went so that I was alone and bathed in darkness.

I fingered the golden locket at my heart, a gift from Tony in our first year together. It was empty inside; I hadn't put anything in there.

I got up and went into the bathroom, where I stuck my head under the faucet and drank directly from the tap. My hair and face dripping, I went back to bed.

We were together for many years, Tony and I.

For many years, I was barely alive.

We breathe the dead in, every day; they're in the dust we kick up, the drifting pollen in the spring. But I was not truly dead. I hadn't disappeared into smoke or memory, as the dead so politely do.

I was a ghost who no psychic called out for. Every day I willed myself into being.

That night I slept on the floor. I dreamed that a sedge of cranes came for me. I grew tinier and tinier, until I was a small bird, nestled on their backs, and I felt only relief as they lifted me from the earth.

***

The airport is miniscule; they pull a set of steps up to the plane and we disembark, right onto the tarmac. It's dark still, but less so–the sky is beginning to hint at dawn.

Daryl takes my hand and leads me away from the airport, toward the fields we'd flown over. The sandhill cranes are there, hundreds and hundreds of them. They're all shadow, all light. They seem not to have bodies.

"Oh," I say, and it comes out all breath, no voice at all.

The cranes are dancing. One of them, in the center, larger than the rest, is leaping with abandon.

Daryl and I watch. He is smiling and I cannot breathe. "I'm going to go look over there," he says, and points at a clump of oak trees gathered atop a small mound.

I nod.

As Daryl walks away, the great crane approaches me. He comes right up, looks at me, and bows, bending his twig legs at the knee and dipping his head.

I bow back.

The flock surrounds me then, circling me like a dance, and the four closest to me spread out their wings and bend their legs and I lean back into them and spread my own arms: and then I'm up, lifted into the air as if I were a dancer myself. I lie back, into the bed made for me by these four wings. Their feathers are greasy and coarse against my bare skin, and I can feel the trembling tension in each wing.

The biggest crane, the one who'd bowed to me, who I now think of as the leader of the cranes, is outside the circle. He's bouncing, leaping straight up, jumping higher each time: first five feet, now ten, now twenty feet in the air. The cranes holding me are trembling more violently, their wings twitching so quickly I can feel the bones within them, and the motion gets faster and faster until I can't feel the bones at all, as if the wings were an engine vibrating beneath me. The leader calls out suddenly, a great whistling chirrup. The whole flock answers back as one, their voices coming from all around me, and then we're up, we're in the air, we're flying.

The cranes remain in their circle formation as we rise, and the four supporting me stay close together, their wings beating smoothly as one. The motion is no longer jerky or tense; it's as though I were lying on a comforter stretched tight in the air, rippling gently up and down in the breeze.

I glance back at the ground, but there's a circle of cranes below me, and I can't see Daryl at all.

We fly in this way until the sky evens out into a clear perfect blue. Below us, the scrubby brush turns to rippling water, which becomes a huge sheet of lake, still and dark. The wind is sharp and cold. My skin prickles. There's a whispering in my ears, the sound of something, some voice—but the cranes are silent.

Please come home. Please come home.

The wings supporting me grow more fitful in their movements and then my feet tilt downwards and we're headed towards the earth. We land on an island—a sandbar, really, though it's big enough to fit maybe fifty people.

The cranes set me down gently. The sand is cool and damp, clumping between my toes.

On the other side of the island, perhaps thirty yards from me, is a little girl, wearing a pale sundress. I tug at my own skirt. I want to call out to her, to ask her if her skin has goosepimples like mine. I don't. I watch her, and she watches me, but we don't wave and we don't move. The cranes are making a ruckus overhead.

Suddenly, the cranes are all above the girl. They circle her: once, twice, three times, and then, as I watch, the child turns grayer and grayer. Her skin turns grainy and the grains soften into a powdery dust, and then, for just a moment, she holds her form: she is a child-shaped sand sculpture. And then she crumbles. The dust settles into a pile, some of it skimmed gently off the top and carried away by the breeze.

I look around the island and I see that there are dust piles everywhere. The whole island is dust.

The cranes are whistling and calling and chirruping and they are rising over me and I realize suddenly what they mean to do to me.

And now: I hear in the winds, the sound again. It's not the whining call of other ghosts, but my own voice, or God's voice, or my mother's voice—is there any difference?

Come home.

The leader of the cranes approaches me. The flock is still rising overhead, and I know that at his signal they will begin to circle.

Three times and you're out.

The great bird raises his beak. It's sharp, I can see that now. He lowers it until it's even with the locket at my throat.

The cranes above me begin a slow circle. Once around.

My neck feels heavy, as though it's being pulled into the ground by the weight of my necklace, as though someone had hooked a rope around me and tugged with all their might.

The cranes begin their second circle. They're calling to each other.

Over their cries, over the sharp hissing of their beating wings, I hear the voice again.

Come home to the body you live in, the skin that stretches for you, the bones that hold you, the joints that bend for you, the blood that flows for you—for you. All of this is for you.

The birds don't react. I don't think they can hear it.

And then I get it.

I pry open the locket and a flood of water, thick with algae and scum rushes out, splashing against my bare legs, my feet.

The leader of the cranes lets out a sharp cry and then he opens his beak wide. I unfasten the golden chain and drop it into his beak.

He swallows it whole.

The flock lands, chattering. The leader of the cranes whistles and then nods to me.

I climb onto his back, fitting myself between the joints of his wings, and he carries me back to the field, flanked by the rest of the cranes.

The flight back is bumpier; the crane's sharp-feathered wings graze my legs with every beat, and I can feel the scratches forming along my calves. From the air I see Daryl, tiny, pint-sized, looking up, looking for me. We glide downwards, and Daryl grows larger and larger, until he's human-sized again. I tumble onto the grass and stretch my arms up, like a triumphant gymnast. I am human-sized, too.

The crane bows to me and then bounds off to his brethren, stiff-legged and proud.

Daryl has moved to a picnic table nearby. I join him.

See the fog that stutters from the clouds? That is for you. This table is for you, the feel of lacquered wood beneath your fingertips—that is for you. And the ground is for you, the earth soft with rain, and the mud, and the flying birds, dipping in and out of the sky, between the patches of fog—these are all for you.

Daryl is saying something, but I can't hear him. His voice rumbles in my ears like the warming engines of an airplane, and above us, the cranes are flying, not in circles, but in a great dark sheet of wings and legs and beaks. They grow tinier and tinier, until they are just a black spot in the sky, and then they are gone.

The Incident at Women's Town

Lara Ek

Lara Ek is a Hungarian-American living in China. She speaks enough languages for half her fingers (thumbs don't count), is interested in everything, and writes the kinds of things she wants to read: ie, weird speculative things with an emphasis on cultural exploration, the societal impact of novums, gender & sexuality, and ADVENTURE. Check her out at Amazon and at Goodreads to enjoy more science fiction and dieselpunk stories written in 1890's slang, and a few stories that are not!

Sarah shot the emissary on a blazing hot day in the middle of a Cycle. She weren't wrong. He'd got fresh. Only the thing was it was hard to tell just how fresh he'd got acause the girl was dying herself.

Proof, that was what the Men allus needed. Proof, proof, proof. As if it wasn't enough finding the emissary in there every day with the fever patient. On her last legs she was, warm as the sun and breath so sour of sick and starvation your nose curdled as you walked in the door. Weren't a thing to keep you in that room unless you was a doctor, but swear that emissary was in there every day, a-talking and a-touching on her. She weren't even of childbearing age!

Sarah'd tried to do it by the book. The day she'd got back from finding herbs, the blue-yellow columbines down beyond the rivers, she'd rode back that noon and gone straight in the doctor-lady's shop. She'd brought her medicinal flowers in, only there weren't no one in the front room. Sick of wasting a day she coulda had for hunting, that she'd used up just getting these weeds, she'd hopped the counter and gone in the hall. She'd barged into one of the back rooms there, snapping, "got them already, now weight them an be done so I can" and then she'd saw: the emissary, a-lying full length on that bed, on his side, one hand under the blankets; the girl close-eyed and red-faced and mewling.

Well Sarah dropped them flowers and pulled her revolver, held it with its mouth pointing at the ceiling. "You get your hands on back to you, sir."

And what'd got her—why, in the end, she'd shot him—was how he smiled. Oh, how he smiled. He looked a cat with a cream. "You can't shoot me. I'm an emissary."

He might've been a man, and that might've swayed another, but Sarah was bare and she didn't see why any bearer might be above the law.

"You just take your hands on back, sir, an come with me out this room."

The emissary smiled like a mule chewing on briars and slowly–slowly–pulled his hand back. The girl coughed a few times and turned from him, eyes still closed, mouth still puffing fever into the room. The emissary looked down at her, wiping his hand on his pants, and lowered his face to her hair –

Sarah clicked the safety off and pointed the revolver at him. "You just step outside with me, sir."

The emissary looked at her, then shrugged and got lazily up from the bed. He sauntered on round it and past Sarah like she was a wooden post, out the hall. He started to make a break out the back door but Sarah'd got behind him, and she tripped him up so he fell on his chin. Then she'd got his collar and dragged him up, out, and round the building, into the street.

Main Street had people, even in this hot time. Women going about their business in shops and behind walls. Girls with their hats pulled down, wide brims shading them from the worst sun. "Hear me!" Sarah called, in a loud, ringing voice. "Hear me now! I've caught a criminal and I am now about to do him justice!"

It was the 'him' that brought them. Women looked up, came to their doors, stood on their porches. Some even came down and near, pulling on hats or shirts agin the sun. A good few of them wore the white kerchief of bearers somewhere on them, tied round arms or necks, or folded poking out from back pockets–subtle, but so's you knew. Girls came to cluster round. A few raced off to spread the news.

Sarah waited til she had enough of a crowd. She let the emissary's collar go and pushed him so he stumbled a few steps away. He couldn't run–the women saw to that. They gathered round behind him, looks of opprobrium on their faces.

Sarah took a gander at him as he recollected himself. Wearing the emissary's white, he was, white cotton suit that stood well on him and set off his skin nicely. He was a pretty-faced one, but some women liked them like that. Emissaries came young, anyhow. He hadn't got a weapon, which also figured–it was why he was allowed to walk freely in town.

The emissary stood himself up straight, tugged at his hems, and settled himself. He looked up at her. "Well?"

Sarah looked round. "Any willing to jury?" She saw nods, curious looks, excited jumps from the little girls. "All right. I have here a snap jury of more'n five. Do you see this? Is this justice?"

Heads nodded in the crowd.

"Then I will begin it now." Sarah turned back to the emissary. "Emissary!" she pointed at him. "I stand you accused of taking liberties with a girl!"

"Do you now?" The emissary shrugged and checked his nails.

"I do! I accuse you of been taking liberties with her a long time now! That fever patient –" she looked aside into the crowd, where someone muttered 'Clarabell'–"Clarabell! You been in her room most every time I've been by there, you been a-touching and fondling her since you arrived, and today–today you was in there with your hands on her! Do you deny it?"

The emissary's lips curled up in a smile and he did not respond.

"Do you *deny* it?" Sarah said again.

"I was only checking to see if she might be biddable," the emissary yawned. "Surely there ain't no harm in that."

"You check that," Sarah growled, "by asking her *mother,* you whore." Murmurs in the crowd. "You check that by asking another, or by *waiting* til she's of age, and not having at her like she was after you!" Gasps behind her.

"But she was after me," the emissary said. Sarah's gun-arm snapped up, but the emissary waved his hand. "Oh, leave off. You wouldn't shoot me. I'm here to provide you the one thing you women need, at least the bearers of you. I been father of five already, you wouldn't dare."

Sarah gritted her teeth but pulled the gun back. "It'd be justice."

"What's more important, justice or a living child?" the emissary smiled smugly. "You wouldn't shoot me. You need me."

"It is true," the crowd murmured behind her. "We do need a stud."

"We can get another," another woman snapped. "They'll trade. They have before."

"They've at least two others," another voice said. "I've saw 'em –"

"When did you see that?"

"Last Trade—walking around in their whites, they was—"

"Hear that, little man, you're replaceable!"

"But I'm here now, and they ain't," the emissary said. "You want the trouble of going through a whole nother Trade? Or you want to just leave this all behind us and go on? Come now, it don't matter none. She ain't my child."

"-still a girl—"

"But she won't be, soon enough," the emissary said. "Her blood's coming soon enough, an she'll be after me again, right as rain, like as any of you women. Or maybe—" he shrugged. "Maybe it won't, an she'll be bare, an then what's the harm done?"

"The harm is in what you done," snapped Sarah above the crowd. "A child, emissary! A child, she is!"

The emissary just smiled. And that smile, that smile like a mule eating saw-briars, that smile like he done over the girl's own body—

Sarah whipped her revolver up and shot him.

Well, as it so-just happened, the crowd of jury round Sarah agreed with her that day, or agreed it was right and true justice. There was indeed some temporary dissenters—bearers, most of them, using the emissary's face and figure to argue it a waste, killing him right there, instead of getting a last ride before shipping him back off to Men's Town, or to the Center for justicing—but not a one of them disagreed that justice had needed to be done. Even the mayor, as she arrived and was told the story, took up longside Sarah.

"Though I'll warn you this," she told Sarah that night at the tavern, huddled in a corner of the bar for quiet, "Men's Town, they ain't gonna like it. You shot one'a theirs, an no matter how right you was–an I ain't saying you ain't–they'll be after you in the next Trade. You just watch."

And sure enough, that next missive from Men's Town called for a justicing at the Center.

It couldn't be right away, of course. Those out on the hunt'd just called back in with a new-bagged screecher and two whole wurms, and anyone hale and able had to head on out and pick the meat from them now and early afor the scavengers descended. They lost a week on that, picking the meat and returning to town, then another in preparing it, smoking and salting and pickling and stuffing the rest in the town's freezer, as full as it'd have. Meanwhilst, the girl Clarabell died of her fever, and without opening her mouth none on what, exactly, the emissary'd done with her. They lost another week interviewing round, gathering evidence and compiling interviews from the girls the emissary'd had his hands on. There was more than one. Women's Town got angry at that, all of them, and there was some missives back and forth with Men's Town raising some serious ideas.

Finally, though, there weren't no more putting it off. On another blazing hot day in what'd been forcibly turned into Between-Cycles, Sarah, the mayor, and a few other women sent a last missive to Men's Town, then rode on out to the Center.

Three days' ride brought them in. The Center was a white and shining building, bright and conspicuous here in the red and purple rocklands. It was one of the few places with a wide enough flatland to commodate a shuttle, so a shuttlepad was set up there behind it, up on the butte, radio towers belled and electric-fenced agin wildlife.

They made it in good time afor sunset. That was a piece of luck. The Men from Men's Town didn't arrive in til after, and looked as if they'd run their horses hard the last few miles. Sweating and bad-tempered they was, all the same but the colors of their skins. Men's Town allus did send the same Men to deal at the Center. Big ones, arrogant ones, stolid, with weathered faces—nothing like the emissaries, who were a varied lot but mostly young, and mostly good-looking.

But for emissaries and pictures, most Women never even got to see what a Man looked like, and prolly the same on the Men's side towards Women. It weren't a wonder the emissaries was so popular—the center of every Trade, and the reason for Cycles.

The Men came up past the labs and into the second-floor courtroom. Center-folk chivvied them over to their fenced-off side, then set up guards along both Women's and Men's fences, blank-eyed, heavy-vested, and hands casual on their belts, close to their guns.

They were mostly bearers. This much time inside and anyone would be. Asides, Center-folk had to bear more Center-folk.

"Ready?" the Judge said. That one was neither man nor woman, a type you didn't hardly get out in the Towns, and if you did they got snapped up by the Center soon's they was identified in the womb. They was perfect as Center-folk: couldn't be said to be biased Men's ways nor Women's.

The Women took their eyes off the Men, turned forward, and nodded. The Men took their eyes off the Women, turned forward, and nodded.

"Then," the Judge said. "I'm here to justice the case of the shooting death of Davie-of-Mora-and-Avery, by way of execution by Sarah-of-Maisie-and-Jem. To recapitulate the case, though I'm sure of it you all know it by now, Sarah alleges that Davie was handling the young girl Clarabell-of-Vella-and-Bryce. As it's known, the handling of any not yet childbearing age is a fatal crime, and the shooting of Davie would then be a lawful one. Sarah, aught to say on this?"

"Yes'n," Sarah nodded, and came forward. She launched into the whole of it, sparing nothing, not a single revolting detail. The Judge nodded after they finished.

"Have you proof? Women, open speech."

"The proof of witnesses ain't come along," the mayor said, taking up some papers she'd brought. She kept one and handed two to a guard, who gave one the Judge and one the Men. The Judge bent over the paper. The Men crowded round theirs, lips moving as they read.

"These are eyewitnesses as seen Davie round not just Clarybell, but a number other girls. Additional to that, he took awful fond to the younger bearers, without an eye for the older."

"Ain't hardly a surprise," someone muttered from the Men's side.

"Order!" the Judge snapped. "You *will* shut your mouth, Jessro-of-Alvina-and-Avery, else I'll have you out this Center! Am I clear?"

The man the Judge'd yelled at nodded.

"Then," the Judge said. "There's witnesses. That's clear. Aught from your side, Men? Closed speech, Women, open speech, Men."

There was a bit of a huddle-and-whisper on the Men's side. A good bit of argument was cut off, and a few smiles and frowns and muttered invectives. Then the Men broke up and turned forward, and one came to the fore.

"We have come to an agreement an accept this evidence. Davie allus was over-eager for his time, an anyone arguin it weren't in him to take to those ain't old enough would be lyin to himself." He looked back over his shoulder. "Love for a brother ain't make it right," he said to one of them, then looked back at the judge. "Still, it's justice been taken out of his brothers' hands an essecuted by an outsider." Here he turned to look at Sarah. "An that ain't right, neither. So we'll be taking her life for the Trade."

Ten Women snapped and sware at once, an ten Men snapped right back at them, an there was cussing an carryin on without pause til the Judge turned up the mic and overrode them all. "WILL YOU BE SILENT," they ordered, and both sides recollected themselves and backed off. Little muttering left, but nothing that the Judge, mic still on, couldn't talk right over.

"Aside that interruption. Men! Have anything more to say?"

The Man in the fore was sweating with frustration. He nodded. "As I was *goin* to say, but I weren't done. We do understand the justice she done—"

"It's a sickening thing," an older Man averred behind him, and the Man at the fore looked back, then nodded out of the way. The older Man stepped up. "Bein a son of Men's Town, we did have love for him, but so heinous a thing as he did—I did read the missives," he nodded at the mayor, then looked back up at the Judge. "Nobody should be left alive of doing such a thing, an were he at that in our own Town, we'd've dealt him justicing our ownselves."

The Judge nodded.

"So," the older Man looked back to the Women. "We'd overlook the strictest life-for-life only in the case of two-for-four Trade, an a new Cycle. Give it a tie-out and two-for-four, an we'll call it a fair justice."

The Judge looked over to the Women's side to see if this was going to be contended, but the Women were silent. Not a one of them looked at each other. They knew what was being said, here.

"So?" the Judge prompted. "Would this be acceptable to the Women?"

The Women but looked once at each other. Then the mayor stood forth, and nodded.

"Then justicing cleared, and passed." The Judge struck the gavel down. "Now, if you can speak without getting your backs up, you may parley the terms. Open speech, both parties."

Trade terms was set to the usual. Two-for-four wasn't the fairest of fair, but it weren't unusually bad–and there was enough Women back in town eager at the idea of trying some Men out for a Cycle that it was all able to be talked out with only the minorest of wrangling.

Of course, Sarah didn't get to see none of it: immediate the justicing concluded, she got taken down to the lockup out back. That was outside the Center walls, though not outside the fences, nor past the Fence: evidently clear anyone getting locked up out here wasn't valuable enough for them to waste their precious chemicaled air on.

It was all right, though, considering. No one took her belongings, excepting her gun and knife, so Sarah out with a deck of cards and laid out a patience game to keep herself occupied. Quiet and peaceful, with just a Center lady–probably a lady, couldn't tell clearly in the protective gear–to watch over her. The mayor and the other Women got to see her a few times along the proceedings, allus bringing news on how the doings went. It got boring, cooped up, so Sarah perked up anytime someone's shadow crossed the outer door. That always meant a good half-hour of talk. All and all, and given the deal, it weren't so bad.

Eventually it come to the end of the dealings; the mayor did a last visit to take her farewells, and wish Sarah well; most of the other women came, too. And as night fell, Sarah settled in to a penultimate evening of reflection and just waiting.

And then come the afterclap.

Center-folk'd just taken away her dishes–awful good chuck for a prison, went down all right and stayed down–and turned on the blue safetylights when there came a knock. Real quiet knock, too, like it was hoping there wouldn't be no one there. The Center-lady went up to the outer door and talked for a spell before finally letting that someone in.

That someone was the new emissary.

And how queer that was. Sarah left her spot on the bed and came on over to the bars, but the emissary hurried forward, "don't, don't stand up for me, it's all right!"

Well, she wasn't going to sit back down, but he stopped outside the bars as the Center-lady sat herself back down at her desk. Just stopped, outside the bars, and hesitated, looking at Sarah.

"I spose you're wondering why I'm here, aren't you?"

Well, sure, she was, but it looked like he was going to answer that for her.

And yes: "well, I just wanted to talk to you, really. I'm the new Emissary, one of them, anyway–but I spose you know that, don't you?" He looked ruefully down at his clothing. Wearing the whites, of course, nicely fitted and well-dolled-up—well, of course they'd want an emissary to look as sweet as he could. This one was a little taller, a little meatier, with an honest, pretty face the bearers'd like, once they saw him. That skin might be honey-colored in the daylight.

"Anyhow—please! Please sit. I do feel like I'm entertaining, here—" and he perched on the bench outside her cell. Sarah sat herself back down on the ground, and waited.

Didn't have to wait long. "I'd just—really, I just wanted to ask, I wanted to see what—what kind of woman could, could do that." Was he blushing? "I thought I'd see, I'm curious, you know. I wanted to know before I went an lived there. I mean—all the other women're—well, you know, they're older, the ones you sent here, but I saw that picture of you they put out, an I thought, I thought—well, she's too pretty to kill someone, that couldn't've been her—"

He petered out under Sarah's stare. "You disbelieved I'd shoot a man on account of how I *look?*"

"Well—well, I don't know—I mean, I mean I do know, I do believe he'd do something like that, I knew Davie, he always was talk-ing about, about—" he *was* blushing, and tripping over his words, now, "about *women* an their *parts* an what he'd like to, you know—but—well, it wasn't what I—I ain't surprised at *him*, just that a woman would do something like that. I mean I don't think they should, should, you know—"

And that sentence never got finished, even with Sarah looking on. Just petered out into blushing and floor-staring. So she leaned back against the cell wall. "Believing in a pervert but not in the justicing. You're a queer little bird, right enough."

"I know." The emissary looked down. "They're always telling me. That's why they're sending me off, stead of Chuck. He's a better stud, by the tests, but they wanna keep him back for something important. This' just a minor Trade, an accident, like."

He fell silent. That got Sarah all-overish. Just a few minutes of his yammering and she could already tell that silence meant bad news. A little girl doing this, she'd be two shakes from bawling her eyes out. Did Men bawl their eyes out? She didn't know. She'd never talked to a man this much before. Hell, she'd never talked to a man before—not talked proper, nothing more than a passing word. How did you talk to a man?

"Here," she said. "Chin up. You'll do fine. You'll see, you get into town an there'll be girls making a mash on you in no time flat."

"They might," he said, not sounding like he believed it. "Anyway, they kept me up here long enough. Done some shuffling in my genes so's I can produce better, fitter, they said. Asides, I like the idea of a woman, steada men. So I guess I'll do alright."

"I reckon you will," Sarah agreed.

How *did* you talk to a man? Sarah waited a bit, but he never said anything, and it didn't look like he would. Didn't leave, though. So she was just reaching her cards out when he piped up:

"Just don't think it's right they're going to kill you."

Sarah looked up sharpish. He didn't know?

"I mean, it weren't what you did," he kept on. "I mean, it was, you did, you shot him, but—given circumstances like that, I wouldn't blame you, I guess. I mean, I know. I knew Davie. I just don't— I don't see why you'd have to die for this Trade to go through. I mean, there's no feud anymore. Hain't been since before my fathers. Men's Town, Women's Town, we're civilized, we got the Agreement, we got our laws, so why do *you*–"

He didn't know! The poor boy didn't know they'd done her a deal!

He didn't know–and she couldn't tell him, not here. Not in the Center, where they'd be recording every whisper. Center upheld the laws, and if they were playing at lawfulness, she couldn't spoil it.

So she stood up and reached out between the bars, to grasp his shoulder. "Don't you worry, now. Don't you worry about me."

He looked up, and there was a funny look to his face. Sarah let him go, but he stood up as she did.

"I'd like it if I could invoke First Night with you."

Sarah frowned in perplexion. "Why?"

"We–well, you're, if you're," he stepped closer to the bars, "I do-," he stopped. He shook his head, and then looked at her again. "I been soft down on you since I saw that picture. There was a picture they sent, on the records. It ain't glamourous, an I guess it's plain, but you–I just-" he took in some breath, "if you're going to die, I'd like, I'd like to try you–"

"You're plumb cracked," Sarah said, and laughed with how strange it was. "I'm not even a bearer, I ain't had stirring toward women nor men since I was born, I got the romantical sense of a hitching-post, an you–you saying you fell for *me?*"

He nodded, watching her intently. "I'm saying that."

She couldn't help it. She laughed again. Just in bewilderment, and at the idea of a bearer–no, not for Men, the Men called them generatives. A generative! A laughable word, for a laughable, pro-creative fancy.

"What d'you aim to get out of this?" she asked. "I *am* bare, you know. I got nothing you want."

Bearers and generatives. Folks who could make more children. Who could keep this planet alive. Where did that leave people who didn't want to procreate?

The emissary looked down from her face to her body, then down to the ground. He stepped back. "It's all I can offer you," he said. "An I'd like to."

In the rest of the jobs. As everything else. As people living for themselves, what they wanted to be.

Sarah was a hunter. She was an explorer. She was a woman who'd rode out, far out, to the deep blue sea. Didn't matter none that she didn't want to make it with anyone. She'd done enough of her own to be worth something.

The emissary took another step back, then turned. Sarah said, "wait."

He turned back.

"Could be interesting. Something I never done." And she nod-ded. "They probably won't let you in here, but you can try. Talk to her," she nodded out at the Center-folk lady. "See if she opens the door. What's your name, anyway?"

The emissary smiled, slowly, like sunrise over the rocklands. "I'm Ira."

It took a powerful bit of convincing to get the Center-folk lady to let up the bars to Sarah's cell, her chief logic being that Sarah'd just killed one emissary, and who was to stop her from doing in another? Ira finally talked her round, though—Sarah thought the lady's finally given in just to be shut of his pestering—and he finally got in, and the Center-folk lady off outside to give them some time private.

He got to doing things. It weren't bad, nor particular good. She was mostly indifferent, excepting when he got so familiar she felt ticklish and uncomfortable, and had to tell him to stop. He backed down on a dime, though, never did never did try to incommodate her. Never did get fresh, just touchy, and clearly he did love touching. It was interesting—she could see how a woman who liked this might like a man or woman who could provide it. A nice passtime, if one wanted that. The most comfortable thing was when he fell asleep on her, head on her stomach, arms round her back; then Sarah herself cricked her legs more comfortable, threw her arms behind her neck, and leant back to sleep herself.

The next morning, they told him to leave. Like a dog with his tail between his legs, he did.

The day after that, they brought her to what was supposed to be her death.

Center-folk took her out, bound her hands, then walked her down along the Fence. Two tall, pale-blue-slatted fences either her; rolls of concertina around electrified wiring along top. A long, egg-blue tunnel, up and up the slopes, all the way up til they came out onto a tiny dais, just a couple rounds of electric wiring round it, a post in the center.

Center-folk took her up there, tied her to the post, and left.

And that was it. Exposure, here, to do the rest. Animals, maybe. The rocklands were good places for screechers' nests. They'd wait til she was dead, or near enough, from the sun and the wind and the starving, and then swoop on down and pluck her apart.

That was what was supposed to happen. It probably did, to some. There was bleached bones about.

Sarah leant back agin the post and waited.

She waited. The sun was fierce, but she was dark-skinned enough it weren't painful so much as bothersome. The wind was fierce, but that was just to be expected, up here. The thirst grew fierce, and ah, now that she had to wait through. She could, though. Some purroot'd be nice to chew on, so she wouldn't dry out entirely, but—well, they didn't put her here for her comfort.

She could see out, far out, unobscured, both sides of the Fence. Funny—only place you could see the Men's Land and the Women's Land both was at the place they both sent you to be killed. She looked out along the bordeau-and-red rocks, the long swipe down into valley, then up again into mesas out in the distance—and the pale-blue line of the Fence, running a straight shot down the center of things, white Center-buildings strung along it like beads.

It was a clear day, and long. Near after sunset—bright and blazing, the sun getting round and orange in a clear sky so dark blue it looked like deep ocean—near after sunset, she saw some figures riding. Off on her left, in Women's country.

It took til fussed dark for them to reach her. The mayor and two others—Tabitha and Bridget, looked like. With them, an extra horse—Sarah's own. Those two didn't say nothing, just climbed off their horses, pulled out horse-blankets and hemp ties and rubber gloves, and set to making the wiring surmountable. Meanwhilst, the mayor scrounged in her saddlebags, then come up behind them, waiting til they could all wrangle their way through.

They did, in time. Tabitha got the cuffs off. The mayor went along the far side of the dais, and left a couple little-barrels forn-ent the edge. Then they all made tracks, left the post out there pointing like an empty finger at the great streak of stars.

It was only after an hour's ride that they mayor spoke. Sarah was on her own horse, with her saddlebags packed as if for a long hunt out in the wild. They'd been delivered to her like that, and now she rode, waiting to hear the deal.

"A year," the mayor said.

Sarah nodded. A year sounded right.

"Three barrels hard strap. Hardest of the hard, could last 'em most of a year if they're miserly. And we got a new Cycle out of it."

"How d'you like 'em?" Sarah asked.

"There's one's a finical one," Tabitha told her. "Likes 'is dressing up, 'e does, likes hearing 'e's pretty. He *is* pretty, sure nough. Got a nice handful. He's no fun, though. Just lies there, like, doesn't try unless 'e's getting his. The other–"

"The other's a right bit of fun," Bridget grinned.

"Got a nice mouth on 'im."

"Sweet, yeah. Very sweet. Tries anyone, bearer or not."

"Though you should know," the mayor chimed in.

Sarah nodded. Well, here was luck, then. A year out in the rock-lands–she could do that. She could do that on one leg. Live off the land and the animals. Maybe explore a bit, if they wanted mapping done. And after a year, she could go back–Men's Town none the wiser, like they played at–go back home to Women's Town. Maybe have another go at Ira. Maybe not.

A year on her own, in the warm wilds. Under the burning stars, as the first moon rose over the rocklands, she smiled and started planning.

Like a Bell Through the Night

Kayla Bashe

Jaffa Volkovitch knew many things. Prayers and curses in antique Yiddish. How to pick the latest fingerprint-coded locks. The phone number of a busty lesbian dominatrix who hosted tasteful orgies out of her Brooklyn apartment.

She also knew that young immortals still aged, up until nineteen or thereabouts. But she had never really considered that people still aged at long distance.

For instance, she'd known Rihannon for a decade, and Rihannon sent her secure letters by messenger blue jay. Most fairies liked bluebirds or sparrows, but Rihannon was always writing long letters and enclosing things: pressed flowers, fabric swatches, ticket stubs. Over the decade of their friendship, her childish tiptilted scrawl had straightened into something that passed for penmanship. She'd gone from wishing for a puppy to walking dogs after gym class to studying dog grooming at vocational school.

But when Jaffa pictured Rihannon, her mental image never changed. A preteen girl in overalls, with dandelions woven into her messy brown braids.

On her third day camping in the Target parking lot, the blue jay landed on her rearview mirror, clutching a single scrap of paper in its beak.

As her seat shifted to an upright position, she blinked at the bird.

Too lazy to reach for the controls, she rolled down the window with her toes. "What the fuck do you want?"

The bird squawked at her and poked her hand.

"All right, all right," Jaffa muttered. She unfolded the paper.

Three words, in shaky glitter pen: I'M COMING. HELP.

It was evening, and she'd just awoken. Her head still pounded from last night's hangover. Her mouth tasted like shit. But the only things in her mind were denim and dandelions. She hoped like hell the girl who wore them still survived.

It had always been easy for Rihannon to lose her grasp on human paraphernalia—concepts like time, numbers, entropy. When she was nervous they skittered away from her like tiny silver fish in a sun-dappled stream. No, like shrapnel after an explosion. Which makes me the walking wounded at the heart of the blast.

The streets around here had so many numbers. I'm a faerie mage, she wanted to tell every sign, not some sort of mortal scientist! She'd had to backtrack three—no, four times. And the overwhelming fear crowding around her like smog didn't help.

The dead, wilted roses in the graffiti-covered planter raised their pink-curled heads in a sudden flourish of vivid life as she hurried past. The unlit sign above the nail salon sparked into full illumination. This injured city was pulling at her, drinking her life-giving power, and it thrilled her to give.

Except I carry power the way a nuclear reactor carries energy. I'm the most precious commodity on the black market. And unlike a nuclear reactor, I don't have security protocols—I don't have guards.

Just me, in the unwashed clothes I scrounged up from my

bedroom floor yesterday morning like the responsible mortal adult I am.

The Copa was playing on a large TV over the bar, a blurry electronic crowd shouting about penalty kicks. She knew Jaffa came here to drink shots of cheap human alcohol and occasionally meet with contacts, that she'd be here tonight. But where was she? She ordered a glass of red wine; when it came, she sipped it cautiously, trying not to wince at the bitter taste.

A white man in a polo shirt sidled up to her. He put his hand on hers. Look unconcerned, she told herself. Odds are he's just some guy—just some human guy from Rutgers on a Thirsty Thursday out...

"You're going to leave with me," he murmured.

Shove off, she would say. I'm waiting for my boyfriend. But by some alcohol-slurred alchemy, her intentions weren't realized. She blinked up at him, feeling sleepy; smoke played around the edges of her vision, and colors shifted in and out of unsaturated dimensions. His hand on her lower back seemed to stretch—were those claws scratching at her shoulder blades? "Uh-huh," she heard herself mumble. He helped her to her feet.

Someone save me, she wanted to scream. The words only came out as slurred little whines. She concentrated, bringing her magic to bear on the fog in her thoughts.

"You want to know what I put in your drink? As soon as I get you to my car, none of that will matter. I'll make one hell of a profit turning you over to the Zagan Syndicate."

The Zagan Syndicate. Allies of the winter fae and the bone demons. They'd spent years sending people to look for her. Even though they didn't know where she was, they could still ruin her life. He herded her out the door and into the dark parking lot behind the building. She managed to plant her feet.

"Come on, sugar girl," he said—like a boyfriend trying to get his girlfriend to forgive him after a fight, as if he wasn't planning to profit from her death. "Let's just get in the car, yeah?" His hand tightened on her shoulder, dangerously strong.

"Hey." Sound spilled into the cold night as the door swung open; a tall, dangerous figure stood in that circle of illumination. "I don't think that girl wants to leave with you." She shifted forward, a predator's walk.

Even drugged and half-dazed, Rihannon still had to catch her breath. She'd remembered Jaffa as being utterly mesmerizing. Childhood recollection hadn't done her justice.

She'd mentioned her age once—early thirties. By human terms, that was middle aged; to shifters, Faeries, vampires, and their kindred, who could live to be four hundred years old, they were both barely legal.

A figure-hugging black tank top showed dangerous cleavage; her jeans left nothing to the imagination but whispered even more fantasies from the way denim poured over her long, well-muscled legs. She wore an old leather jacket like battered armor, and the streetlight showed every scratch.

The vampire scoffed. "Who the fuck are you?"

"I'm the dumbass with nothing better to do than take you down." Her mouth twisted, and fuck-you Crimson lipstick accented that wicked smirk, dark curls as glossy as a blackbird's wings brushing against her shoulders. "But you can call me Jaffa... ring any bells?"

"Dammit," he growled. "They said you were dead."

"Funny how rumors spread."

They lunged at each other and began to fight, bloodsucker speed and agility against pure bestial instinct and strength. It was almost too quick and intense for the human eye to follow. But suddenly Jaffa stumbled, and the vampire took the advantage, grabbing her by the throat.

The drug had worn off, and Rihannon sprinted forward. "Get away from her, you jerk face!" She swung her backpack at his head, and her full water bottle banged his skull. It took him an instant to process the pain. In that moment, Jaffa stabbed him. A wound through the chest would slow any immortal down for at least a week.

Her hand came down on Rihannon's shoulder. "Hey. Kid."

Rihannon blinked up at her. "You knew I was in there?"

"I have a decent memory for scents and faces... and I could hardly forget yours. You all right?"

"I'm a little shaken up, but nothing that won't heal. Do you still have that motorcycle? We need to get out before this creep's backup arrives."

"My baby girl's been in the shop these past few weeks. We'd travel faster on her, but right now—we'll just have to make do." She gestured to a nearby beat-up car. The movement made her wince, and Rihannon noticed.

"Oh, no. Are you badly injured?"

"Just a scratch. Come on. You want to take the wheel while I bandage these up?"

"Umm... I'm kind of a shit driver."

"You're, what, twenty in human years? Must've had plenty of practice."

"It's not safe for me to drive when I'm in fae mode. I keep thinking about the caterpillars chewing through their cocoons in the oak trees and the dandelions blossoming at the side of the highway. It's only my magic that lets me avoid crashes."

"Note taken. I'll get us onto the highway, then—we shouldn't be seeing any cars once we're far enough from civilization."

Jaffa lived out of her car. It wasn't as if she didn't have the money to own homes. She just liked being able to move wherever the job took her... or flee when she felt the Zagan Syndicate nearby. The tradeoff was that her car was a fucking mess. She shoved some of the magazines with article titles like BEAUTIES OF THE NEGEV DESERT and ISRAEL'S HOTTEST QUEER WOMEN into the glove compartment, and kicked some greasy paper napkins under the seat.

Rihannon slid into her own seat and looked around. "There's one thing you've forgotten."

"I doubt it."

Her smile was an infuriating flash of sunlight through clouds. "Seatbelt," she said, clicking hers into place.

"Uh-huh. Tell the immortal shifter to wear her seatbelt." Jaffa shook her head. "I stole the car, I make the rules." She rifled through the glove compartment and came out with a first aid kit.

"Okay. But you should still wear your seatbelt."

How long had it been since anyone dared to tease her? With the slightest roll of her eyes, she pulled the seatbelt across her chest.

Jaffa pulled out of the parking lot. "So... is this a pleasure visit, or are you offering me a job?"

She'd hoped to see Rihannon just because Rihannon wanted to see her. But the little faerie looked worried, her normally warm brown skin ashen, her pretty dark curls limp under her hoodie.

"I need to get out of human territory, now."

"Did you piss someone off?"

"Yeah, by existing. You remember how it's been safer for me in the human world? Well, now the tide's changed. I've got to hurry home, as quick as I can."

In her opinion, unfair was something that weak people said when they were making excuses, but Rihannon's situation really was unfair. A daughter of deposed Fae nobility, she'd been forced to hide in the human world most of her life. She had immense power, and there was no telling what would happen if her magical strength fell into the wrong hands. Now that the rightful ruler was in control once again, it was safe for her to return, but various mercenaries were trying to kill her or capture her for her power before that could happen.

"My aunt said she'll meet me in Connecticut. She has a portable portal..."

"You don't carry your own escape route?"

"Most powerful Faerie mage in a generation. There's no telling where that portal would lead after a few weeks in the same room with me. A high celestial pocket dimension, or the rich dark fire at the beginning of the universe. Sometimes I look at the stars and laugh for the sheer joy of living under them. I could warp a portal's essence and end up on some planet known only to Life itself. I mean, I'd like to be the witchy goddess of an evolving civilization, but... awfully impractical, really." When she laughed, her magic sparked.

Power poured off her smooth skin like waves of pure honey. People would kill for just a taste of this, Jaffa thought. Smash the world up to drink her down slow.

They were reaching an intersection, and Jaffa slammed her foot on the brake a little too hard. "You keep that shield up, you hear me? No telling who might be sniffing around. " With that wild nimbus of power, Rihannon was like the neon sign outside a strip club, broadcasting an invitation to the world.

Instead of shielding herself, instead of being sensible, she just blinked at Jaffa. "But I'm safe around you, aren't I?"

"I'd kill myself before I laid one claw on you, but I'm not unaffected. If you think I can play chauffer, sniper, and bodyguard with all that power curling from your lips like cigarette smoke every time you so much as breathe—well, you'd be right, because I have more control than these slavering idiots who are after you. But it's still damn distracting. You dial it down, yeah?"

"Or what? You'll knock me on the head with a shovel and hogtie me in the trunk?"

"Yup, that's what you young things are doing these days. Bodily harm and kidnapping. Prime material for a new episode of I Love Lucy."

Rihannon settled back in her seat, casting a dubious gaze at Jaffa, who pretended not to notice. "Stop pretending you're all that much older than me."

The first time they met, though, Jaffa had felt infinitely older.

Baby powder and white roses, lemon sugar, sweet honey still in the comb. The light glittery scent of faerie magic drifted over the lawn and kissed each wildflower. A little girl with deep brown curls was seated in the middle of a sunbeam, humming some action-movie theme as she steered a winged doll through a clump of weeds. She wasn't a stock photo or a china figurine. Her hair was tangled and she'd worn through the knees of her jeans.

And Jaffa, lurking in the bushes at the edge of the yard, thought, what a goddamn good kid.

Then the first assassin leaped down from the tree, his gun already raised. Jaffa charged at him. She caught the bullet in her palm, already shifting; she hit the ground in full feral mode, with a snarl that showed every sharp fang.

Within an instant, she'd sunk her teeth into his neck and ripped. Her hands nearly paws, she fought the remaining assassins, heedless of the bullets sinking deep into her fur. "Kid," she whispered, her voice hoarse. Her body could no longer maintain beast form; she dragged herself over on scraped hands, wincing with every movement. "Kid, you can come out–it's safe now, I got them..." For a moment everything was silent. Then Rihannon peeked out from behind a tree. "I knew you'd protect me," she said, her wide eyes shining. "I just knew it." At that moment, Jaffa knew she would have died for this girl's sake. There was a huge element of boredom in looking after someone who lived in the middle of nowhere. Rihannon went to school, to ballet class, and came straight home. On weekends, she and her aunt Anwen went to a local faerie prayer circle. Jaffa, used to high-stakes undercover assignments, thought longingly of New York.

Of course, she'd always been tough; her name was Jaffa, after the city. As a beast pup, she'd been raised by a scrappy Ashkenazi pack of newspaper boys and partisans, still as scruffy and hard-edged as they'd been when their aging slowed down. It was a household where the pantry lead to a secret escape tunnel and every discussion turned into a friendly argument in at least three languages. It was an upbringing that, she thought, had prepared her for anything. Except spending an entire summer in a small Midwestern town where the only place to cut wild was the county fair.

If not for Rihannon, she would have died of boredom, watching shitty reruns on the shoebox-sized old TV all night. Most children were scared of her, but Rihannon didn't care. She invited her bodyguard to play Disney princess death match in the tree-house, brought her to school as a substitute gym class teacher, and whispered hilarious stories about all the backstage gossip of Nutcracker rehearsals. Having someone so interesting to look after helped her suppress the instinct to run wild.

"Tell me a story?"

So Jaffa talked about roaming half-wild in the Catskills, and how she'd stolen a neighbor's chicken for show-and-tell; how she'd followed her foster parents into the mercenary busi-ness, and the three surreal months she'd spent undercover as a mortal fundamentalist to take down a baby-trafficking ring. "You're brilliant," Rihannon always said. "I want to hear more."

At night, Jaffa crouched at the window with her sniper rifle, shooting down the occasional demon hunting party or extradi-mensional mercenary. She left at the end of the summer, when Rihannon and Anwen moved to a safer safehouse and the attacks ended. And although she was damn glad to be around other adults, she still caught herself looking at wildflowers and ballet slippers and wondering what Rhiannon would think of them.

Ten years was a short time in a shifter's life, but it had made all the difference in that sunshiny kid. She'd grown into her power, emerging into near-immortality. The innocent teenager she'd felt so protective towards had grown up—and out—into one sweet little shot of whiskey. And feisty, too.

No more oversized band t-shirts and hand-me-down cargo pants; her current outfit was just as simple, but it fit her body, hinting at generous breasts and hips.

Down, dog. Don't even think about it. This innocent creature was under her protection, and it wouldn't be fair or right to make a move.

She noticed Rihannon was studying her. "So... uh... how you feeling about going back to Faerie?"

"'Tis less-more mad where the glitter woods run, as I might sling syllaslang had I been caterpillared behind the Borderbrook's rush." Her voice fell into the sparkling, singsong tone that young Faeries often affected, half music and half mischief.

Jaffa nodded. "Not bad for someone raised with humans." It was a pitch-perfect imitation, and she couldn't help chuckling.

"All my allowance and birthday money, for my whole life, went on buying smuggled magazines from a secret mailing list. I keep up well enough with the important news and the biggest trends in pop culture, but I don't remember what it's like to feel that bright air on my face or drift for hours in a sunbeam—just a few blurred memories of colored streamers waving overhead, fried pastries, dancers on stilts. I'll wake up every time I hear a bicycle messenger or a unicorn rider because I'm so used to cars—I bet I'll still reach for my phone even though everyone in Faerie wears a communication crystal. In the way I walk, the way I dress, even the weather I'm used to, I'll seem as human as can be. But I've never fit here, either. Could never. Too much magic in my blood, too much flickering Faerie whimsy. I laugh too easily and I eat foods none of my friends have even heard of–I haven't grown up with the same lullabies as them or even the same holidays. Sometimes I feel like I don't fit anywhere."

She'd never thought of her sunny faerie as having problems, but now she knew Rihannon had suffered too. She felt genuine regret for a world that had forced a young girl to flee for her life. "That's real tough, kid. I wish things could have been different."

"I don't." Her dark eyes fixed on Jaffa's. "There was no other way. This way, I'm alive–free to have problems and worry about whether or not I fit in." She tapped her phone on the dashboard, her expression growing impish once again. "And I should be able to pick up some decent money when I sell this at the Goblin Market."

Jaffa wanted nothing more than to swerve over to the side of the road and give Rihannon the biggest hug of her life. She now knew that Rihannon was wise beyond her years, that the trials of her life hadn't made her bitter. There was still something pure in the world. "You're... you're really something, you know that?"

She ducked her head, smiling. If her skin was lighter, she probably would have blushed. Jaffa tightened her grip on the steering wheel, preparing to weather another honey blast of common-sense-melting-magic. Instead, the smile faded.

"Still, I can't help worrying."

"About what?" Jaffa wondered if she could punch whoever or whatever had upset Rihannon.

"If my bits-and-pieces childhood has robbed me of the ability to truly fit anywhere."

Okay. She could metaphorically punch this. For a moment, she forgot her old wounds. "I mean, I was raised by immigrants, and I think of it this way: maybe it's taught you to make friends anywhere. There will be outcasts and dreamers and lonely souls wherever you go. Anyone with your kind of sympathy, who can be kind to people who feel left out... I don't think you'll have any trouble making friends. Show some sympathy for people's shit, and you'll never get shitfaced alone."

"That's actually really reassuring."

It felt strange to have a pretty girl smiling at her. "I'm just telling the truth."

"I know. That's why it helps."

A few hours of starlight later, they were driving across a gravel road in the Pine barons. Jaffa winced at each bump. It had been a while since she'd seen a healer, and her old scars were starting to ache, warning of nearby danger and dark forces. Was there a real threat, or was her body just on high alert for the sake of its own unconscious paranoia? She had no idea.

Rhiannon looked at her, concerned. "Are you all right? You didn't get hurt earlier, did you?"

"Let's just say that the Syndicate... once they've got you in their crosshairs, they don't let up... not until they've had their fun, or they think you're no longer a threat."

"What happened to you?" Rhiannon asked, then shook her head.

"No–I shouldn't be prying. If you're not comfortable talking about it, I understand. You don't have to tell me anything you'd rather keep secret."

It was a mature and selfless response, and she couldn't help but consider how the little faerie had been forced to grow up so quickly. Jaffa had spent years keeping secrets so close to her chest; now she wanted to share a fragment, even if it was just a minor detail. "I ended up on their radar when I stopped a sprite-smuggling operation. They'd taken over some catacombs, rigged a portal, and were selling the little creatures to mortal collectors in glass bottles."

Compassion and concern filled her tone. "That's horrible. I'm glad someone did something about it."

She'd felt the same way, willing to risk anything to end the atrocity. "I thought I'd made it out with my cover intact, but let's just say it was a while till I made a clean getaway."

Rihannon didn't press her for details, just nodded sympathetically, her face solemn.

And if she knew the truth, would she still feel safe in a car with me, Jaffa wondered. She wanted to change the subject, quick as she could. "Anyway, kid..."

"About your last letter!" Rihannon piped up. "I couldn't help wondering–you promised to tell me about the fire-eaters, but I haven't been in one place long enough to summon a bird."

"For starters, let me just say you haven't seen anything until you've seen a flame nymph twirl flames on her tits."

Jaffa wasn't just a brilliant storyteller, she was a brilliant listener. She listened to Rihannon's descriptions of every elderly dog her school had fostered, every quirky customer she had to wrangle with in job placement class. At last Rihannon was too tired to talk, and she curled up in a little ball as Jaffa hummed along to the radio. She didn't remember falling asleep, but she woke up at 3 AM when they pulled into some cheap motel.

"One room, one bed," Jaffa told the sleepy-looking clerk, who blinked in surprise and looked them up and down before shrugging acquiescence to their request.

"Why was she so surprised?" Rihannon asked in the elevator. "I mean, sharing a bed is cheaper, right?"

"There are a lot of LGBT people on the east coast, but this is the cheapest no-name place to get a bed within state lines. It's butt o'clock in the morning, you're walking like you're drunk, and you've got sleep hair. Let's just say gal pals probably didn't go through her mind."

"Oh!" Rihannon covered her face, laughing from the awkwardness. Then she snuck a look at Jaffa. Did she mind that the clerk thought they were sleeping together? Would she want to go out with Rihannon, or did she still just see her as a scruffy kid in overalls?

But Jaffa's face was unreadable as always. Rihannon decided to turn up the flirting a little and see if she noticed.

Okay, it's stupid to flirt with my bodyguard—my biker-chick-sexy shifter bodyguard. But I've spent my entire life being so careful. She'd never even gone on a date because she didn't want to draw too much attention to herself. Now life was offering her the chance to be a normal young faerie, to eat Wing City street food and make flowers blossom in public. Maybe a normal stupid crush on a hard femme who was way out of her league was just what she needed.

The room was run-down, but it looked like it had been cleaned recently, and Rihannon didn't notice any cockroaches or rats. While Jaffa made a security sweep and checked for bugs, Rihannon took her suitcase into the bathroom. Back in LA, her friends had always tried to talk her into dressing more revealingly, saying it would help her snag a hot girl. She thought she'd never wear the vintage slip dress that Sofia had talked her into accepting as a going-away present, but since she'd thrown it in mid-packing-frenzy…

Rihannon stepped out of the bathroom, the nightgown swaying against her legs. She'd brushed her brown hair until it shone in the starlight. Maybe Jaffa would be stoic and unreadable no longer. Even if her flirting made things awkward, at least she'd have a distraction from the constant threat of death.

Except Jaffa was already fast asleep.

Fine, Rihannon thought. Good thing fairies are early risers! She slipped under the quilt and closed her eyes.

The next morning, Rihannon leaned over Jaffa as sun peeked through the curtains. She thought of the brightest, most glittery things she could to make her aura even more inviting: walking barefoot on the LA beaches, the smell of country-fair food.

Waking up my bodyguard in three, two, one…

A hand closed on Jaffa's shoulder. One thought pierced through the fog of sleep: those bastards, I won't let them get me again. She grabbed the person by the throat and slammed them against the wall before even opening her eyes. So the Syndicate thought they could mess with her again? She'd fucking show them.

Rhiannon stared at her with eyes full of fear. Instantly, she released her grip, seething with horror at herself. "Shit."

"You're such a heavy sleeper, I wanted to see if I could wake you..." Rhiannon swallowed hard, touching her bruised throat. The movement drew attention to the low neckline of her nightgown, a silky slip dress trimmed in lace. Did she know how tight it was? Twin dark circles showed through the pastel fabric.

Fuck. Jaffa ran a hand through her hair. Spending so much time around the faerie's unshielded aura was seriously getting to her, like some sort of crazy secondhand high. "I'm a heavy sleeper until I register a threat. If I'd sensed there was anyone watching us, I would have gone from zero to sixty in an instant. You set off a false alarm—it's not your fault. Change out of that and we'll grab breakfast. I'm going for a smoke." Around humans, she smoked normal cigarettes. The tobacco chemicals bounced right off her immortal metabolism, not even touching her racing thoughts; it was another part of her persona. But around other immortals, she lit up the real stuff—elfweed spiked with pixie dust, all charcoal and maple smoke. I could do with one now, Jaffa decided, and got out of bed.

That is, she tried to.

"Are your old injuries hurting badly today?" Rihannon's doe-brown eyes filled with concern.

"No. I'm—fine." She tried to pull herself out of bed and stifled a cry of agony. The spells implanted in her bones hadn't throbbed this badly in months. Evil forces were nearby... looking for Rihannon, possibly. Well, they won't find her here. I'll get her to a safe haven. But first to get out of bed.

"I can't take your pain away, but I can turn a bad day into an average day," Rihannon hinted.

She must have looked dubious, because Rihannon continued. "I know about pain. Sometimes it's worse and sometimes it's better, right? But it's always there. And everyone thinks you should either be in bed crying helplessly or just get over it... but you keep going because you're a fighter. And that's what you do."

In the morning sun, she seemed so old, and yet so innocent. Jaffa wished she'd done more to protect her. "You sound like you know a lot about pain."

"One of my poetry teachers had late-stage Lyme disease. I couldn't get her out of the wheelchair, but I kept her out of the hospital until treatment kicked in. No organ failures on my watch."

"That's all? Really?" She hadn't meant to ask. It just slipped out. But Rihannon sat on the edge of the bed, letting out a small, melancholy sigh.

"Sometimes it sucks being on the run. I've had to leave California behind, switch what I'm studying, even change my name. I just want to go home and swim in the town pool, volunteer a few shifts at the library. I'd ask my neighbor how her rose garden is coming along and Sofia and I could do each other's nails and I could pet Carmen's pugs. Instead I can't even log into my old social media because some greedy technomancer might decide to use my BFFs against me. And it sucks so much ass." She looked straight at Jaffa with a tremulous smile. "But I'm living with it, even though it hurts."

"Yeah, kid. I getcha," Jaffa said softly. In that moment, she would have done anything to make a home for her old friend. One that Rihannon would never have to leave.

Then Rihannon laid a hand on her, and the magic rushed through her like a drug. She didn't know they were moving closer together until Rihannon's forehead touched hers. Didn't know they were kissing until she heard herself moan.

Jaffa tasted like smoke and spice and dark chocolate, and her skin was as warm as blankets and the dawn. Rihannon wanted to melt into those hands gripping her shoulders, into this blissful dizziness. "Yes," Jaffa gasped, and she growled and buried a hand in her hair, as if Rihannon was a tantalizing treasure to hold fast to, as if she wanted to live in this moment forever. She hardly dared to breathe. Jaffa's long hair swept over her, brushing against her collarbones, the swell of her breasts. She heard herself sigh, a deep shiver of untamed sound-

"No," Jaffa said, her voice sharp as barbed wire. "We can't do this. We can't ever do this."

Rihannon fell back against the headboard, her mouth open. Emotions swirled through her: exasperated, upset, confused. "But-why not?"

If she'd been awkward, or angry, or even ordinarily polite, Rihannon would have known how to feel. Instead Jaffa smiled a strange half-smile and chuckled a razor-blade laugh, a laugh that seemed to mock the world as much as it mocked herself. "I'm too old for you."

"You can't say that and really mean it. I'll live to be at least two hundred. Can't you make more sense? At least tell me if you like me or not—or let me know if I'm a bad kisser." Heat flared over her cheeks, and only her olive skin was saving her from a humiliating bright red blush.

"I know the High Fae measure age in full moons because those are the only things they know how to count. But there are other immortals—the extraplanars, the undergrounds... who measure age in what a person's seen. What they've been through. And my soul is older than yours will ever be."

Jaffa said it so matter-of-factly. From anyone else, those words would have seemed ridiculous. But there was nothing of drama or pretension in the contradiction of her smile. She stood up and ran her hands down her body as if to erase any evidence of Rihannon's touch. "I'm going out for a smoke. Get your stuff. We'll leave in ten."

"What about the free breakfast buffet?"

"Fuck the buffet." She slammed the door behind her, and the glass rattled in its frame.

Rihannon took the pillows off the bed and threw them across the room. At least she wasn't a High Fae, so fragile and ethereal that she could barely tolerate the intense vibrations of the human world—but now she could imagine how it felt.

She's still going to see me as a child, the rest of my life.

Something chimed from inside her tote bag. She opened it. It was the burner phone she'd gotten for Aunt Anwen to contact her in case of emergency.

Instead of saying, "Hello," she said "What's the password?"

"Pear juice."

Their password—the recipe for Rihannon's favorite human drink—protected against impersonation.

"Celery and avocado," Rihannon replied, completing the password. "I'm so glad to hear from you! Is everything all right?"

"Yes, but there's been a change of plans. I'm being tracked as well, so I thought it would be safer to meet you halfway. I used magic to trace you earlier today, and I've been driving like a bat out of the demon realms ever since. In fact, I'm right here in the parking lot, can you come down and meet me?"

"I would love to," Rihannon said, and hung up the phone. She glanced towards the glass door, wondering if she should let Jaffa know. Then she decided against it.

Well, let her worry for a few minutes! When she found out, it would make her realize that Rihannon was no child. *I got to the faerie realm without your help, without even bothering to tell you.* She flipped an elastic off her wrist and put her hair up, slung her purse over her shoulder, and left the hotel room.

Jaffa felt like she had confirmed every stereotype by forcing herself on the faerie. The predatory older lesbian, the feral werewolf incapable of controlling her animal lust. Her claws dug through her jeans as she imagined former friends staring at her in disbelief and anger. That was the unfortunate part about being culturally Jewish. You couldn't pray away your wrongdoings with a Hail Mary or whatever. You just had to deal with the guilt.

She smoked deliberately, slowly, her eyes fixed on the featureless forest horizon. At last, all too soon, the worn-down embers stung her skin. With a sigh, she ground the cigarette out under her foot and slipped back inside.

"Rihannon? Where are you?" She glanced in the bathroom–in the closet. The faerie was absent.

Then her phone began to ring. ANWEN, the screen read. She leapt on it.

"Well?"

"Oh, Jaffa, forgive me–I was careless–they've had me in their grasp for days, I managed to escape–but they've gotten the secret password, they'll be able to trick Rihannon into coming to them... they wanted to use me as bait, but I broke out of the car once their truth serum wore off. You must tell her I'm all right. She is with you, isn't she?"

"No," Jaffa said, her voice hollow. As if magnetized, she looked out the window. She saw the faded lines of the parking lot, the head of brown curls bobbing in the sunshine.

The phone fell from her hand as she broke into a run.

Jaffa emerged into the parking lot running at top speed. Then she skidded to a stop.

"Fuck," she heard herself whisper. She'd hoped never to see the Syndicate's torturer-in-chief again.

But now she was here, leaning against a black van with tinted windows. Her blonde curls rippled in the wind as she turned her contemptuous gaze from a helpless Rihannon to the new arrival.

"Well, isn't this perfect! Jaffa Volkovitch!" She laughed, high and lovely as birdsong, and tightened her grip on Rihannon's neck. "They say shifters are proud beasts, but you cowered like a whipped mutt when I'd finished with my skinning knife. Oh, yes, my team and I got everything we wanted out of you–and more, much more. I thought I'd have to dirty my hands today, but you? I know you've learned your lesson. So we'll just be going."

 In any other situation, Jaffa would have been paralyzed with fear. Spasms of panic would skitter up and down her scars, reducing her entire awareness to pain–to what she'd suffered at those pale, pretty hands. The hands of a woman who'd skinned muscle from bone and laughed at the agony she caused.

But now those hands were wrapped around Rihannon's throat. And anger blazed through her mind, wiping away everything else. Letting out a furious roar, she charged.

Fifteen minutes later, Jaffa had propped Rihannon up against a tree. She was washing blue demon blood off the faerie's face with the least greasy of her backseat napkins. In the cold early morning, Rihannon seemed as still as a doll, her eyes wide and unseeing. Jaffa fought the impulse to gather her into her arms and warm her with kisses.

At last Rihannon shook herself, blinking. Then her gaze fixed on Jaffa.

"Was it true, what she said about you?" she asked.

"Yes," Jaffa said, looking away. "Everything she said—and more. Want to know how I escaped? I didn't. They got tired of hearing me beg and left me in a shallow grave to rot. There you have it." She snapped her fingers. "Get rid of your phone; it's been compromised by Syndicate technomancers. I'll hack the car and see if I can confuse them."

Rihannon didn't reply. Still shocked into silence, Jaffa thought with a merciless smile. "See, aren't you glad you didn't kiss me?"

"What?" Her voice was too quiet to hold discernible emotion.

"I know what you remember about me. The protector from your childhood, wearing a supple leather jacket and disappearing in a cloud of backroom smoke. The Big Bad Wolf to your Little Red. I've learned to live with the battle scars, but you, sunshine... I'm worried you've got some warrior princess fantasy lover in your pretty little head. That I'll hurt you when I let you down. See, it's not just that I was in pain. I begged for my damn life. I didn't even escape. They only let me go because I had no more information to give them. Now you know—come on, let's go hotwire another car-" She turned to move away, but Rihannon grabbed her jacket.

"Wait. Do you think so little of me—of yourself—that you expect what you've been through would make the slightest bit of difference?"

Jaffa could always turn her words on a woman. Words to seduce, to mollify, to tempt. Now, for the first time in her life, she stood utterly speechless before a woman she genuinely loved.

"Don't you remember all those letters you sent me? I loved them because they contained stories of your adventures. But what I loved even more was that you cared enough to write to me, no matter where you were. I don't want some made-up perfect woman. I want to be with the woman who would risk her life to save someone in trouble, just like you did today. The fact that you've got a few weaknesses doesn't change the fact that you're the strongest person I've ever known. You think you're protecting me by pushing me away, but do you know where the one place I've felt safe is? Here. The only times I've ever slept through the night, not worrying about kidnappers or goblins or the Syndicate, have been when I'm with you. I've had to give up so much to keep my gift out of the hands of people who would use it for evil… running from home after home, sleeping in anonymous safe houses and Faraday cages made of iron. if you want to protect me, let me have this. Stay with me. Please."

"You mean that? All of it?"

"My magic draws people to me. It doesn't make people want to kiss me unless…" She giggled and shook her head, glancing down at her cheap sneakers.

Jaffa reached out. Slowly, she drew Rihannon's chin upwards. A smile had slipped onto her own face now. It felt so easy it startled her, like walking barefoot on soft grass. She could imagine a thousand more smiles, all just as natural, all reflected in the sweet mirror of those doe-brown eyes. "Unless?"

"Unless I want them to kiss me back," Rihannon said. The words all flew out in a single silver laugh.

Jaffa could think of no better invitation.

Studying the shifter, Rihannon realized that the Syndicate's cruelty had left a hidden scar just as painful as the ones that stiffened her limbs. They'd shoved her into a deep pit of hatred, convincing her that she was unworthy of love or a home. *I can't carry her out of that darkness, but I'll be there to cheer her on when she starts to climb.* "If you want, you could come with me to Faerie. Be my lover, or even just my roommate."

She grinned, with only a hint of sardonic weariness. "You sure about that, kid? I shed. And I haven't changed as much as you have; I still like partying, picking up girls... Just because I've always had a soft spot for you doesn't mean you can change me."

"I'll buy a lint roller. I'd be happy pulling some loose fur off my couches if it meant you were comfortable." *What she really meant was: I don't care if you're not perfect. It's not a burden to cope with you, it's an opportunity to care for you.* "And as for partying, picking up girls, even taking more than a sip of wildflower wine... I've lived in hiding. Haven't talked to another immortal except you for years and years. Why wouldn't I want a little wildness? I wouldn't mind settling down with you, but I'd much rather be wild with you." She took Jaffa's hands. "We can get a first-floor studio down Border way. What do you think?"

"How about this, kid. Let's travel together until we get you clear of human land. Then, once you're surrounded by your own people... if you're still set on me, you can make me that offer again, and I'll know you mean it."

"And what will you say?"

Jaffa let out a low growl of possessive contentment and swept an arm around Rihannon's shoulders. "Yes, you damn little enchantress—yes, if you'll have me. A thousand times yes."

Could yes mean until forever? All Rihannon knew was that the further they traveled, the less she'd worry about where she truly belonged. Because even the open road could feel like home with someone you loved.

An Astronaut Lights a Candle

Megan Neumann

Megan Neumann is a speculative fiction writer living in Little Rock, Arkansas. Her stories have appeared in Crossed Genres, Daily Science Fiction, and Perihelion Science Fiction. She is a member of the Central Arkansas Speculative Fiction Writers' Group and is particularly appreciative of their loving support and scathing critiques.

The candle needed to be put out. I knew this. Still, as I descended the basement staircase watching the flames flicker, I feared the darkness of the dying flame.

The candle burned every night, casting its light against the walls. These walls—the walls of Grandmother's house—had stood through the Blitz when she was a young woman. They stood now in the age of cell phones, Twitter, and Facebook. Grandmother had watched the candle burn and now me. I was the last watcher of the candle. I would be the one to put it out.

I had been building my courage to step into the basement for nearly three weeks. Each night I'd swallow a glass of red wine and step onto the staircase. I would stand, simultaneously experiencing the light of the candle as well as knowing it couldn't possibly be there. Its existence was impossible. I would wait for the footsteps and the shadow. As soon as I sensed the presence of another in the basement, I would turn away, close the door, and try to forget what I had seen. There was no candle and no man in the basement.

***

I was five or six when my grandmother took me to the basement for the first time. We were in the kitchen, me propped up on a stool by the bar and grandmother standing before me, her face long and serious. She seemed ancient to me. I realized now she was probably only in her late forties, the age I am now.

"Siobhan," she said, "your mother is gone."

I nodded. Mother had been gone for some time, though I didn't know the exact amount of time. It could have been months or just a few days. Time didn't mean much to me. My days consisted of playing in the garden when it was sunny or playing in my room when it rained. I only knew mother had vanished one day. It had not alarmed me. Maybe she had gone on holiday. Eventually, it sunk in, becoming a fact like the sky is blue or fire is hot—Mother was gone, and I would not see her again.

"Your mother has left us, child, and it's not such a bad thing," Grandmother said. "She was not always here when I needed her. Or when you needed her, for that matter."

I nodded again, more for show than understanding. My mother lingered in the background of my life, sometimes scolding, but mostly indifferent. I never needed her. It was Grandmother who fed me, clothed me, and told me when I could play in the garden.

"She couldn't handle the responsibility of this house. Because she is gone you'll have to take on her job much sooner than I wanted." She paused, as if expecting an answer.

This time I didn't nod. I didn't understand Grandmother's words. I remained silent and nervously tugged at my jumper.

"Look at me, Siobhan."

I looked up. Grandmother's eyes were wide, blood shot. I concentrated on the lines of blood lacing across the whites of her eyes. These lines terrified me. Would they burst? Had they always been there? Or had they only developed because Mother was gone?

"I'm going to take you to the basement today," Grandmother said. "I'm going to show you what it means to take over this house. You might be scared, but know I'll protect you. You needn't be afraid of anything you see down there."

The basement—I had never been allowed. Grandmother said spiders lived down there and large rats as well. This was enough to deter my curiosity.

Night had fallen when we stood at the basement door. I held her hand loosely, but when she pushed open the creaking basement door, I tightened my grip. The glow of a flickering light filled my vision.

She led me down the stairs, each step creaking. At the base of the staircase, I saw a small table with a single white candle held by a brass candleholder. Fat drips of wax ran down the side of the candle like sweat. The plain wooden table did not seem out of place, and I idly wondered why my grandmother would leave a candle burning.

"What were you going to show me?" I asked.

"Wait." She placed a hand on my shoulder and dug her nails into my flesh. This hurt me, and I let out a small gasp, tried to pull away. "Wait," she repeated. "Watch the candle. Look at the table it sits upon. What do you see there?"

"Only a candle burning," I said. "Why did you light it? Is there no bulb?" I glanced up. A single bulb with a long pull string hung from the ceiling.

"Watch!"

I started to protest, to run up the stairs, but a gust of wind brought my attention back to the table. The candlelight was gone. The basement was shrouded in darkness. A ground level window let in a small amount of light, and I could make out the shape of the table. The candle was in the center of it, not lit, the wax new and smooth with no drips down the side.

I pressed against my grandmother. I wanted to close my eyes but a loud pop, a sudden flash of light, made me look. Then he appeared.

I assumed it was a he, though I didn't know. Some form of human stepped from behind the table. He wore a white suit, similar to suits of the astronaut that had walked on the moon a few years earlier, though his suit was slimmer, harder looking, not as puffy. The helmet over his head was made of a smooth reflective glass. The images it reflected were not of the basement, not of me and my grandmother, but of a dark stone room.

I whispered to my grandmother, "Who is he?"

"I don't know. But he cannot hear us. Cannot see us. He is in another world."

"Is it a man?" I asked.

"I don't know."

Years later, I realized she didn't mean man or woman, but rather, she did not know if he was human.

He leaned over the table and picked up a book of matches. He struck a match against the book and lit the candle. Then he lifted his head as if hearing something in the distance. He dropped the matches, backed away from the table, and something lifted him into the air and pulled him away into the dark hole that had formed behind him. The candle remained lit and the hole disappeared.

I learned this scene of the candle being lit repeated daily. After the first day, my grandmother showed it to me, I refused to see it again. I cried in my room alone, weeping for the man who was pulled into darkness.

"We should help him!" I told Grandmother.

"Nothing can help him. We can only observe."

She didn't know what would happen if the house were destroyed, but she feared it could be disastrous. On her deathbed, only about twelve years after I saw the candle for the first time, she said, "There is a thin membrane between this world and his. Whatever pulls the man into darkness could pull all of us into it. We must protect the window, keep the glass from shattering and letting darkness in."

I inherited the house when I was barely an adult. I gave up on the idea of university, a real job, or moving away from London. I needed to stay in the house, to watch the candle and guard the membrane. I was protecting the world from darkness, or so I told myself.

Often in the night, however, I'd wonder if any of it was real. Sometimes I would stand at the top of the staircase, reminding myself there was a candle.

People offered to buy my house, developers wanting to build new condos. I turned them down. I could have taken the money and bought a nice little cottage out of the city. Maybe I'd have taken a job at shop or a pub. Anything would have been better than staying in the house with the candle burning in the basement.

Thinking my grandmother wished this upon me brought up a great anger within me, turned my body hot, and made my mind incapable of coherent thought. I wanted to destroy the house. Take a sledgehammer to the basement and smash through the walls. I wanted to bury the astronaut. If such an act destroyed the world, so be it. The world deserved destruction. It deserved nothing more than what I'd already given it.

Other times I felt a sense of pride knowing I had a secret. This secret kept the world safe. In some way, I was a hero. Siobhan Harris—superhero.

All these thoughts came to me late at night. They faded as daylight came. Then I'd go on with my job down the street—an assistant in a bakery. I never bothered learning much in school, knowing I would never be able to go far. A woman could do many things in London. But the house called, and I couldn't abandon it. I didn't want to be far from it for any amount of time. What if someone saw it? What if a robber broke into the house and touched the candle?

The world would be gone in an instant—maybe.

Or maybe nothing would happen.

Why risk it?

Now I had to risk it. I had to face the astronaut.

A few weeks after my forty-seventh birthday, my doctor diagnosed me with pancreatic cancer. I was very ill, he said. I'd felt poorly for some time but never bothered with taking care of myself. When I finally went in, he said I had nine months—maybe. If I kept up with my treatments. I should get my affairs in order, he said. Tough business, cancer, he said.

I decided not to keep up my treatments. I would die alone in my house, as my grandmother intended. Perhaps she wanted me to have a family like her. Maybe I was to have another daughter and force her to live in the cursed house.

I'd never inflict my curse on another generation. The curse must end with me. I knew as soon as I died, the house would be demolished. It was an outdated, poorly maintained blemish on an otherwise modern street. The roughness of the destruction would ruin whatever delicate boundary existed and the whole world would be destroyed. Everything my grandmother feared.

Of course, I didn't really know this. Grandmother never really knew. But I felt it in my heart. She must have felt it as well. We were given this house and place for a reason. The reason must be as protectors. Before I died, I would enter through the barrier, disrupting whatever loop trapped the astronaut. I would do it safely, without destroying the world. That would be the end of it.

After three weeks, I gained my courage to finally sit on the floor of the basement and watch the astronaut closely. I noticed the subtle movements of the man. When he came into the room and found the matches, he paused glancing around the room quickly, as if searching. His hands fumbled with the matches, nearly dropping them more than once. He shook as he lit the candle. What else did he expect to be in the room?

My own hands were shaking the night I decided I would slip through the barrier. I told no one, didn't say goodbye to anyone. I didn't expect to come back through the barrier. I would most likely be sucked in with the astronaut. Or I would cause the end of the world. I didn't know, couldn't know. I was dying though, so what did I have to lose? I was ready to find out the truth, even if it ended my life a bit prematurely.

I waited for the candle to go out. This happened between 6 and 8 PM every night since my grandmother was only a girl. She never mentioned if anyone else in the family had known of it. Had my grandfather known or even my father? I had known neither of them, and they were never mentioned. As I stood waiting to step through, I wondered if they knew and couldn't stand the secret, couldn't live with knowing such a thing existed. Only a woman could keep a secret like this for so long, only an English woman could hold something so tightly to her heart without ever loosening it.

The whoosh happened suddenly although I expected it. It always occurred suddenly. I didn't hesitate. I stepped toward the table, expecting some kind of sensation as I passed through, but there was only a drop in temperature and a change in the smell. I smelt dampness, wet stone. My breath fogged in front of me. A shiver passed through my body.

I realized I stood on something other than the smooth concrete floor of the basement. It was dirt and gravel beneath my feet, making crunching sounds as I walked. Then the astronaut was before me. I saw myself reflected in his helmet's glass face. Close to him, I saw the suit was stiff, a hard white plastic. I knocked the candle from the table, ending the cycle. Then I reached out to touch him. As my fingers grazed his mask, a light flashed.

***

I awoke in a white room. People swarmed around me, at least six or seven men and women I didn't know. They spoke at once, their words incomprehensible.

A woman with loose black hair cascading over her face held out her arm and shouted, "Everyone! Get back and shut up!" She moved close to me. "Are you all right?" she asked. "Do you know where you are? Do you know who you are?"

"Siobhan Harris," I answered. "I don't know where I am. I was just at home a moment ago."

The people turned, looked at each other.

"Siobhan Harris?" the woman asked. "The Siobhan Harris who lived at 14 Lorne Road."

I nodded. "That's me."

The woman shouted at a man behind her, "Help her out of here! Let's get her to the clinic."

The man started to lift me, but I felt suddenly dizzy.

***

I was lying on a small cot with a rough blanket covering me. Sitting in a chair across from me was the same woman from before. She was reading a book, but when she saw me sitting up, she closed the book and set it on a table beside her.

"You're awake," she said.

"Where am I?"

"That's going to be difficult to answer," she said, her words slow and deliberate. "You won't believe me, but I want you to remain calm and know I have no reason to lie to you."

She stood, walked to the edge of the cot, and sat. I should have felt uncomfortable by her closeness, but I didn't. I needed this closeness, needed to feel another human near me. It had been so long since I'd talked intimately with someone else. I hadn't realized my life was so isolated, so focused on the candle in the basement.

"I'm Dr. Preeti Ramesh. You asked where you are. That is difficult to explain, and yet, the answer is very simple. You're home. You're at 14 Lorne Road."

"I don't—"

Preeti held up a finger.

"Please, I'll explain. You're at the same place you were before you woke up here. However, you're not in the year 2016. It's 2085."

I started to stand up, but Preeti pressed on my shoulders.

"Before this morning my colleagues and I thought Siobhan Harris was dead. She disappeared nearly seventy years ago. The people who knew her had no idea where she'd gone, but her doctor reported she was dying from cancer. So maybe she'd gone to some beachside town in the Bahamas to live her last days. That's what people liked to believe. But I'd always suspected, she'd done something else with herself. I was right, wasn't I?"

This was a rhetorical question, I suspected, so I said nothing.

She went on, "After you disappeared, a developer wanted to build condos on this block. They had your home declared abandoned. When crews went in to demolish it, something strange happened."

Preeti paused and smiled. "The debris of the demolition began to disappear. Walls of plaster and wood gone, as if it had all been sucked up by a big vacuum. This continued to happen. When certain government agencies heard of it, they took over. Everything was covered up, and their best scientist set to work. They discovered an anomaly, a bubble of space and time that did not belong. Although invisible to the human eye, this bubble when breached absorbed whatever came into contact with it. Where did these things go? No one knew.

"For two generations we've been working here, trying to understand it. For that long, we've had nothing new from it, no better understanding, until today. Do you know what happened today?"

Preeti looked at me, but I had no answers for her. I didn't even know what day it was, let alone what had happened.

"You happened. You appeared on the floor just outside the bubble. When you watch the videos from the monitors, you can see it. The bubble forces you out. Plops you on the floor. When the bubble opened up, we could see inside of it. Do you know what we saw?"

This time I did answer. "You saw a room. A stone room. With a candle on a table?"

Preeti nodded slowly. "That's right. That's exactly right. What is that room? It's not your basement. The basement was made of concrete and brick walls."

I shook my head. "I would tell you if I knew."

Preeti came closer to me, took my hands in hers, and said, "Tell me everything you do know. Nothing is too mundane."

I looked at her dark, smooth hands clutching mine. Then I told her everything. I started from when I was a girl, how my mother had left us, and continued on to the point I crossed the barrier into the stone room and kept the astronaut from lighting the candle.

When I had finished, Preeti squeezed my fingers. "Thank you for sharing. You need more rest and maybe a bite to eat. I can have something brought up to you or you can come down to the cafeteria and eat with us."

"I think I'd like to be alone for now."

"Of course. There'll be some food up here soon. Then you rest. We can talk again tomorrow."

"I'll be here."

"You're not a prisoner here," she said. "You can leave if you like, it's just—"

"It's just I have nowhere else to go. I'm already home."

***

The next day Preeti took me to the basement to see the bubble. It was unrecognizable as my old basement. For one thing, the table, candle, and astronaut were gone. They must have vanished when I breached the seal seventy years ago. The concrete and stone had been replaced with new white flooring, and most of the white walls were lined with desks with computers.

She showed me the tests they ran daily and the data they'd been gathering for years. None of it made sense to me. I thought often during her tour I was dreaming. I had fallen asleep in the basement and imagined all this. Or I was still a child, and Grandmother had yet to show me the secret lying in the basement.

"You can see most of our data answers nothing for us at all," Preeti said. She held a sheet of paper with columns of numbers beneath my face.

"This all means nothing to me."

Preeti dropped the paper and said, "Of course it doesn't.

Honestly, it doesn't really make much sense to me either. I've gathered nothing useful in all my years here. I've created a lot of charts about changes in pressure, but what has that gotten us?" She laughed and smiled a close-lipped smile.

"Then why even bother with this." I motioned at the center of the room, where presumably the anomaly lay. "Whatever this is. There's so much life beyond this tiny space. I spent my whole life dedicated to protecting something which has absolutely no meaning. I thought it would destroy the world if I left it alone, but no. It's nothing. If it has an answer to the question of its purpose, I'm sure the answer is its own insignificance."

Preeti shook her head. "I can't believe that. I believe understanding this will change the world."

"Don't waste your life like I did," I said. "I'm not going to anymore. I'm going to leave."

I turned to walk up the metal staircase, which had replaced the old wooden stairs of my home.

"You don't have much time left!" Preeti shouted after me.

I turned mid-step.

"We ran scans on your body yesterday. You don't have much time left. Your cancer, there's a cure nowadays. We can send you for treatments. You could be well by the end of the week."

"Why would you do that?" I asked.

"Help us understand the anomaly. You're the only one to have spent so much time with it. You're the only thing to have come out. That must mean something."

"It means nothing. My grandparents just bought a house in the wrong spot." I started up the stairs again and didn't look back. I found my room with the cot and tried to gather my things to leave. But nothing belonged to me. The closest thing I had to my own was the hole in space in the basement below.

There was a knock at the door, and Preeti entered.

"Stay," she said. "Let us cure you. Not for the bubble, but for your own life." She came toward me and took my hands in hers. I should have pulled away, but I felt comforted by her.

I looked into her golden brown eyes and decided I would stay.

***

Preeti hadn't exaggerated about how easily I could be cured. The facility brought in doctors and treated me in my small room. My cot was exchanged for a hospital bed. After a series of intravenous treatments—which made me feel awful for three days— I was, according to my doctor, completely cured. I could live another fifty years if I watched my health. But what were fifty years in this strange world with technology I didn't understand? Such a life would be miserable, but then Preeti started staying with me. During my treatments, she pulled my sweaty hair back when I needed to vomit. She was an angel while I was in hell.

I was in love with her, but I couldn't tell her, couldn't say it aloud. Thankfully, she did it for me.

When I had recovered, she took me to her apartment and asked me to stay.

"I think you know how I feel about you," she said on my first night out. "I think you feel the same. So why not stay with me? You've been alone your whole life. You don't have to be anymore."

So I did, and I wasn't alone for the first time since my grandmother died.

Preeti showed me the latest in London life. It wasn't much different from what I had left. The cars had changed shape a little. Some new shiny buildings had been erected. The old structures—the Tower of London and Parliament—looked exactly the same.

Most nights during dinner, Preeti ranted on about the bubble, what it meant to science. Sometimes she would get especially scientific, and I would look at her with glazed eyes. Then she'd sigh and shake her head.

"We're talking time travel. Openings in space and time," she said one night when she was particularly excited. "Moving great distances through the universe in a short amount of time. If we could only understand the bubble and apply what makes it tick to our own technology. That must be pseudo-science enough for you to understand."

"Maybe I do. Maybe I don't. Or maybe I don't care either way."

"What do you care about?"

"You," I said, smiling. "The portal is amazing. You're right about that. But it's only amazing to me because it brought me through time to you. It's a love portal."

Preeti laughed. "That's a good theory on its purpose, better than our own at the lab."

"What's your theory?" I asked.

"You're not going to like it," she said, looking down at her plate. "We think the bubble is just a fluke. A disruption in an otherwise well-functioning universe. Like a paint chip on a shiny new car. But what a fantastic disruption it'll be if we can learn the things I've talked about."

She was right. I didn't like that theory. I grew sullen, knowing I'd spent my life worrying over a fluke.

***

Over the following weeks, Preeti's colleagues interviewed me, ran tests on my body. They asked questions about the basement, about the "astronaut," and about the candle. They wanted to know the type of candlestick, the details of the metal. What color was it? What did it smell like?

"It had no smell," I answered. "Only the smell of a cellar. Dampness."

I was sure nothing useful came from my answers, but I wasn't bothered. I only wanted to be near Preeti, to complete the life I was lucky enough to have.

Then Preeti told me some interesting things were discovered after my arrival. The bubble expelled trace amounts of my DNA on a daily basis—fibers of my hair or bone.

"That's creepy," I said. "What does it mean?"

Preeti stared at me, frowning. "I think it means you're still in there."

***

Although Preeti was trying to act normal around me, I could tell something was wrong. After the discovery of my DNA, everyone at the facility started acting strangely. It made no difference to me if bits of me were flying out of that damned bubble.

But other things were happening as well. Throughout the day at the facility, I'd hear alarms blaring in the basement, people rushing about looking harassed. No one ever spoke to me about these problems, and I didn't care enough to ask.

Then one evening Preeti rushed through the front door of our apartment, her eyes wide in panic. She hugged me. "I won't let them do it."

"What?" I asked.

"They'll come, and they'll try to take you, but I won't let them."

"Who'll try to take me?"

Her eyes were unfocused, fearful. "We need to get out of here!"

She rushed to the bedroom, and I heard her open the closet door. I could tell from the noise that she was pulling things down from shelves quickly.

"What are you doing?" I called after her.

I was about to try to calm her when the front door opened and two men came in. One held what looked like a gun, but not quite like any gun I had ever seen. He pointed it at me, so I held my hands up.

"Siobhan Harris, come with us."

Behind me, Preeti had rushed out of the bedroom, sobbing.

I thought they would take me to some hidden bunker or prison cell, but instead, they took me back to the facility, back to my old room with the cot. They locked the doors. In the back of my mind, I thought Preeti would rescue me. She would come for me and save me as she had saved me from my cancer.

I fell asleep on my cot and awoke to Preeti standing over me.

"You're going to be okay," she said, but I could tell from her voice things were not okay. "We've had a meeting, all the board attended. I didn't get to speak, of course, but everyone agreed they can't force you to do anything."

"What are you talking about? Can I go now?'

"No," she said and let out a great sob. "Siobhan, they won't ever let you leave now. You're too important."

I started to make a sound of protest, but she interrupted me.

"Let me explain." She took a deep breath. "We've been developing probes to send into the anomaly for years. We've sent many models through, but it's always been futile. As soon as they go through, they're gone. We never gather any data from them. But in the last few months, we had a new model we thought would work, a different kind of signal that we believed would be strong enough. We were going to send it through last week, but it won't go."

"What do you mean it won't go?"

"Nothing can go into the bubble now, except—" She stopped speaking and took my hands in her own. "Except pieces of you."

"Pieces of me?"

"We realized nothing could go through at the same time we realized things were being expelled—your DNA. And I didn't tell you, but the fragments of you were old, as though it had been floating around for a hundred years. Then some of the other doctors had an idea—they thought if you were coming out, then maybe pieces of you could go in. They started to send your blood samples through. And when they did, the sample containers came back out immediately, but they had also aged."

"So?" I searched her eyes and realized I knew the answer.

"We've never been able to get readings inside the bubble. That's really what we need. So they wanted to send you through to get those readings."

"I won't go," I said, sitting up.

"You won't!" Preeti said, pushing on my shoulders. "We already agreed that no one could make you. But they want to keep you here for samples. Send your blood through, laced with tiny robots to record everything."

I sat down again. "Okay, so I just provide a sample of my blood every once and a while? That should be okay."

"It will take some time to develop the new sensors that can go in your blood. Until then, they want to keep you safe here."

***

For several weeks, I lived contently in my little room with the cot. Eventually someone brought in a better bed, and Preeti brought items from her home to make it feel cozy. We ate dinner together in the cafeteria, and I tried to stay positive. My life was still better than before. I had Preeti. And even though alarms were going off more and more in the basement, I rarely thought of the astronaut and the candle.

I thought Preeti was happy too until one night when we were eating dinner the alarms went off again. Only now the alarms blared in the cafeteria as well. Everyone stood and rushed from their tables toward the exit.

"What's going on?" I asked.

"Something's happened to it," Preeti said.

I followed her down the stairs to the basement where dozens of people stood at the perimeter of the room staring at one wall. Immediately, I knew why they were staring—a wall of computers had been ripped out, revealing crumbling dry wall.

In the center of the basement, I saw a shimmer of something flickering.

"It's volatile," one of the onlookers shouted.

Preeti shouted back, "We need to put in another sample, but we can't get close enough! We need to drop the perimeter!"

She sidled across the back wall and placed her hand over some kind of screen. A light flashed on it and then I heard a loud thud. I looked at the center of the room. A huge metal box had fallen from the ceiling and encased the bubble. The alarms died.

***

"I didn't tell you how volatile it was because I knew it would upset you," Preeti said.

"What else haven't you told me?"

"Well, it also only calms after a sample of you has been sent through."

"But why?" I asked, stunned.

"We have our theories." Then she became silent.

"What are they?"

"We think it's expecting you. That it requires you to go back in to set something right. It knows you're out of your time, and it needs you to go back in."

I sat on my bed shaking. "This doesn't sound like the behavior of a fluke, a disruption. What happens if it continues growing as it has been?"

Preeti opened her mouth, but no words came out. Tears fell down her cheeks.

"It'll keep growing until it can't be stopped, won't it?" I asked.

She nodded.

I sat for several moments rubbing my arms and shivering. Then a calm came over me. "I'll go in then," I said. "What choice do I have?"

"We could keep trying to contain it!"

"There's not enough time," I said. A sense of peace came over me, as if this decision was the first right one I had made in my life.

***

I nearly collapsed to my knees when they showed me the suit with the sensors, the suit I'd wear into the bubble. It looked like an old astronaut's space suit, but it was slimmer, made of hard plastic, not as puffy.

"You'll be tethered, and we'll try to pull you back once thirty seconds has passed," some faceless scientist said to me. "The sensors will be on collecting data while you're there."

I nodded solemnly.

"What will it feel like when I'm there?" I asked Preeti.

"We don't know," she answered.

"Will I die immediately?"

"We don't know. You might not die."

"When you pull me back, if you can, a hundred years will have passed. I won't be alive. That's how all my samples have been."

"It might be different," she said. "We don't know."

"Cheer up. Think of all the data I'll have collected," I said. "Think of how the world will be changed by it. Do you think that was the point all along? That's my theory."

I slipped on the suit, which made my body bigger, mannish even.

I approached in the center of the lab.

"Siobhan, try to make contact when you pass through," another scientist said. "Press the button on your wrist to speak to us."

I nodded, but I knew I would not speak to them ever again.

Then I stepped through.

Around me, the stone room was finally complete. It was an old cellar, probably built in the eighteen hundreds by the looks of it. I couldn't see too well, so I approached a table in the center of the room. I knew a large box of matches would rest on it. I struck the match against the book and lit the candle. I could see the lights of my sensors inside the helmet recording each moment. I looked around nervously. Would I be taken back?

I felt a pull backwards and then blackness.

I was in a room, a cellar. There on the table was a candle. I needed to light it again. The sensors continued recording.

Blackness.

I needed to light the candle again.

I lit the candle again and again. How many times? Hundreds. Thousands.

Each time I appeared, I realized my fate again and wondered if it would be the last time or if it was the first time.

I never grew tired, never felt anything other than the desire to light the candle and do what had to be done. How did I know it had to be done? Because it had already been done. I had witnessed in my youth. My grandmother had witnessed it as well.

I moved toward the candle, but this time it was different. I heard a pop. An arm knocked the candle from the table and then reached for me. I looked up and saw a tired woman. She touched my face, and I felt myself pulled back for the final time.

Thank You

Many thanks to our patrons
and supporters, especially:

Natalie Weizenbaum

Cathrin Hagey

Tory Hoke

GriffinFire

Want to see your name here? Become a patron!
patreon.com/lunastation

About the Cover Artist

Priscilla is an illustrator with a focus on covers and portraiture. She bears a deep love of games and books, particularly of the sci-fi and fantasy stripe. Past clients include TOR, Fantasy Flight, Uncanny Magazine, White Wolf, Onyx Path, Hi-Rez, and more. She's also been featured in ImagineFX and the Society of Illustrators West. She's currently traveling the world, seeing the sights.

Contact her at priscilla.h.kim@gmail.com for any inquiries.

Learn more about Priscilla and see her work at:

www.priscilla-kim.com